SPORTING

KYLIE GILMORE

Cover design by: Michele Catalano Creative

Published by: Extra Fancy Books

ISBN-13: 978-1-64658-025-5

What's a little kidnapping between old friends?

1

Eli

As one of Summerdale's finest in blue, I'm not supposed to say that people are idiots, but tonight has really tried my patience. So far on my shift, I've:

Caught minors with alcohol (five times). *Could you at least take your crap beer into the woods where I don't patrol? Get a clue!*

Confiscated illegal fireworks (three times). *Can we not blow a finger off on my watch?*

Explained why people can't park in an emergency zone (too many times to count). *Idiots.*

The irony is, I used to be one of those idiot rule breakers. Who better to enforce the rules than the guy who broke them all as a teen?

My shift is over, so why did I come back to the center of all the action at Lake Summerdale? Tradition. It's the end-of-summer regatta—everyone's out on the lake on boats with festive lights—and I wanted to watch the fireworks with the community I grew up in and love. I'm on the shore, out of uniform in a black T-shirt and jeans, leaning back against a tree to soak it in. There's nothing like a warm summer night by the lake. So many memories here with my family, enjoying a picnic on the shore, swimming, fishing with my dad. Later, the lake was my go-to place for making out with girls. That was before I came up with the brilliant idea of stealing a car to drive to a more secluded spot for all my amorous activity. No license either, but I was a quick study.

I stand and stretch as the fireworks come to an end with one final burst of brilliant red, blue, and purple. Always a good show from the town rec department. I linger onshore, letting people clear out ahead of me. No reason to rush to the crowded parking lot over at The Horseman Inn just to sit in my car. Though my new car is a beauty, a silver Ford Mustang GT premium convertible with heated leather seats, V-8 engine, and 10-speed automatic transmission. I've had her two weeks, my first new car ever (the rest have been used), and she's been a dream to drive.

Finally, the crowd thins, and I make my way along the curving lakeside path to the road. It's close to a full moon tonight, and the silver of my Mustang glows in the moonlight. I washed her earlier today, using a special polish for a final touch, and she's looking fine.

I cross the road, pull out my key fob, and unlock the car. The rear lights of a red Honda Accord parked in front of my car light up.

No-o-o. I watch in horror as the Honda backs right into my brand-new Mustang. I suck in air. The crunch of the Mustang's front bumper feels like a personal hit to the solar plexus. My baby. My brand-new baby.

I rush over to inspect the damage. The front bumper is destroyed.

I gesture angrily toward the driver still in their car. "What the hell are you doing? You backed into my car!"

The door of the Honda opens, and a familiar tall blonde woman steps out. Jenna Larsen. She's my older sister Sydney's best friend—my onetime teen sex fantasy—looking hot as hell in a snug white T-shirt and jean shorts that show off her long legs.

None of that matters at the moment.

"You ruined my car!" I shout, gesturing to the unforgivable damage. My pride and joy that took many paychecks to cover. And the car's not even paid off!

She glances at me before walking over to inspect the back of her car. Not my car. *Hers!* Like her rear bumper is the bigger issue here!

I gesture to my front bumper. "Look at this! It's brand new, only been off the lot for two weeks!"

She looks at my dented bumper. "Calm down. It's a little ding. I'm sure they can fix it."

I can't take how casual she is about this atrocity, especially after the exhausting night I've had. "Did you even look before you backed up?"

Her eyes shift to the side, appearing mildly guilty. "I have a backup camera. It just wasn't working for a moment because I pressed the radio."

I stalk closer in full authoritative cop mode, right into her personal space. She's only a few inches shorter than my six feet, and we're nearly eye to eye. I keep my voice level. "And you never noticed the backup camera fails to work when you start pressing buttons?"

Our gazes collide, and something changes, a primal recognition of one body to another that steals the air from my lungs. *Is that lust in her eyes?*

She licks her lips, and the blood rushes through my veins. She shifts away abruptly. "I'll pay for it, okay? Just let me know how much." She gets in her car and drives off.

I run a hand through my short hair, dazed for a moment. I've known Jenna for as long as I can remember. She started coming over to the house when she was five and I was three. Other than a long horny period I went through from thirteen to fourteen (okay, fifteen) where she starred in all my sex fantasies, I've barely given her a second look. I moved on to girls my own age, who didn't see me as Sydney's annoying little brother.

Back then, my mischief-making was in fine form at Sydney's slumber parties with her three best friends—Jenna, Audrey, and Harper. I'd steal their snacks and hide around corners to scare the crap out of them. They'd get so furious at me, except Jenna. She acted like I was a mere inconvenience to an otherwise fine time. She'd pat me on the head and send me on my way. Which is to say she never took me seriously.

Whatever. I'm over her. She moved back to town last summer to open a bakery, which I never visit because I avoid sweets. I haven't been avoiding *her* for a year. That would be ridiculous. We just haven't run into each other, until she literally ran into my car.

I slowly turn back to my Mustang, focusing on the important thing here. She ruined my brand-new still-not-paid-off Mustang. Even if they fix it at the shop, she'll never be the same.

My older brother Adam calls out to me, gesturing toward my car. He's with his new fiancée, Kayla, looking happier than I've seen him in a long time. "That sucks. You've had it, what, two weeks?"

"Yeah."

My mind flashes back to Jenna up close and personal. Things are different now. I'm twenty-seven to Jenna's twenty-nine, and the years don't matter much between two fully adult bodies.

I blink a few times. Dammit, I still have a thing for Jenna Larsen.

Jenna

I do *not* have a thing for Eli Robinson. I tap the steering wheel rapidly as I drive home, fresh from our fender bender. That was just…a weird moment. A weird angry alpha-male moment—his eyes hot on mine, his sexy earthy scent, the deep timbre of his voice. A hot shiver races through me at the memory.

Up close he didn't feel like the Eli I grew up with. How is it I never noticed how filled out he is? Thick with muscle from his corded neck to wide rounded shoulders. He used to be a skinny scrappy kid. Now he's got five-o'clock shadow on his square jaw. I knew he grew up, of course. I've seen him around town, doing his cop thing. Sometimes I see him from a distance at The Horseman Inn, the historic bar and restaurant that my best friend Sydney owns. He plays acoustic guitar occasionally on Saturday nights. I never got up close though, eye to eye, a breath away. There was something about his bristling authority as he confronted me that turned me on.

Gah. I can *not* be turned on by Eli Robinson. He's Sydney's irritating little brother. Worse, Sydney's overprotective of her two younger brothers, Eli and Caleb. She helped raise them after their mom died when she was twelve. Eli was ten and Caleb eight at the time. With her two older brothers, she's hands off—they helped raise her. The two younger brothers, she's a mama bear with. Still.

Sydney and I are as close as sisters, joined at the hip since kindergarten. And that sisterly bond means a lot to me since my own sister dropped out of my life. Fallout from my parents' nasty divorce.

Okay, so no more weird thoughts about Eli Robinson. He's not a guy I could ever be with casually, which is all I can handle. Sydney would freak if I did. She knows exactly why I avoid relationships. I don't have to look any farther than my parents' horrendously drawn-out divorce to know a committed relationship isn't for me. Even so, I did try a couple of times to make it work with a guy. My longest relationship was a month in college. When the guy wanted me to meet his parents, I felt like I couldn't say no, but it was too much too fast, so I broke up with him. He got clingy after that, trying to win me back, and the harder he tried, the less I wanted to go back to him.

Then there was the time I *really* tried with Brian, a year after college, but it ended after three weeks when he said I was always distant. I didn't see that at all, which only made him feel sorry for me. He said I was incapable of being close to someone, and I believed him. The evidence was staring me in the face, after a long history of nothing ever working out for longer than a month. I just stopped trying. The problem is me. I'm not relationship material.

I get out of the car and walk to the separate side entrance

to my apartment over the bakery I own, Summerdale Sweets. I took over the old café in town from one of the original hippy founders, Rainbow, last summer. I'd previously lived in Brooklyn, commuting to Manhattan for a soul-sucking job in IT. I miss the lively dating scene of Brooklyn. Here it's harder to meet single guys. Summerdale is mostly families or guys I grew up with, like the man who's currently pissed at me. Men and their cars. I'm sure they can fix it at the auto shop no problem.

I go straight to my bedroom, plug my phone into the charger on my nightstand, set my small purse on the floor next to it, and head into the bathroom to get ready for bed. Other than the shock of running into Eli's car, it was a blah night. I know I shouldn't let it bother me, but of my three best friends—Sydney, Harper, and Audrey—two of them are married now. Only Audrey and I are single, and she's determined to find her Mr. Right sooner rather than later. I don't begrudge my friends their happiness, but I've known for a long time that marriage isn't for me.

Now that my closest friends are getting married, probably starting families soon, I can't help but think they're going to leave me behind. They'll move on to new married-couple friends or mom friends, and I'll just be the second-rate "aunt" they invite to their kids' birthday parties.

I brush my teeth vigorously as I rethink my life choices. Maybe I shouldn't have quit my job in IT. It paid well.

Maybe I shouldn't have followed my passion for baking back to my hometown.

Maybe I should just leave.

To go where? To do what?

I spit out toothpaste and rinse. I don't know why I'm so unsettled. Here I am having a quarter-life crisis on a beautiful summer night after enjoying the moonlight regatta with friends. It's basically a floating party—all our boats tied together on the lake—with fireworks. It was a good night, all things considered.

I change into my summer pajamas of an old T-shirt and sleep shorts and climb into bed. I close my eyes, and the accident comes back to me. The jolt of my car hitting something. The jolt of Eli up close. Then another memory comes back. A sweet one. Eli stopped by my house the day I was leaving for college in North Carolina. He was sixteen, not filled out yet, but tall. As soon as I answered the door, he thrust a bouquet of red roses in my hand and told me he'd miss me. I thanked him, and he left just as quickly as he arrived. At the time I was surprised but thought it was a nice gesture.

My phone rings. I turn on the nightstand lamp and lean over to check the screen. It's a local number, but I don't know who. *Eli?* I flush hot, my heart pounding for no reason at all. Just because I felt the tiniest bit of lust one time doesn't mean I can't talk to the man. It's just Eli.

I let it go to voicemail.

After a few moments, I hear the notification and pick my phone up. A text pops up.

Hey, it's Eli. I got your number from Sydney. Let me know your insurance info. I'm taking the car into the shop as soon as I can get an appointment. Here's my info.

There's an image attached of his insurance card. It's nothing personal, but my heart won't stop racing. Why does texting feel so intimate suddenly? Is it because I'm in bed?

I unplug the phone, prop myself up on the pillows against the headboard, and consider what to text back. *Sorry I missed your call and ruined your new car? Long time no see?* He's never visited my shop, and I've been there for a year. It almost seems like he's been avoiding me. Everyone I know stopped by within the first month.

I'll just call. This is so not a big deal. I click on his text, and the phone icon pops up. See? Easy. My finger hovers over the button. *Just press it.* Adrenaline fires through me. I press the button anyway.

"Jenna," Eli says brusquely in his deep authoritative cop voice.

I hang up.

Crap. I set the phone back on the nightstand and stare at it. Maybe I should just turn it off. I can call him back tomorrow and say we got disconnected because my phone died.

The phone rings, and I grab for it, accidentally knocking it to the floor. I scoop the phone up and jab it a few times, so eager to recover from my earlier hang-up that I manage to hang up on him again. Dammit. Now it looks like I'm avoiding him. I've known Eli practically my whole life. Well, there was a big gap there from when I left for college and didn't come back until last summer. The gap where he morphed into a gorgeous swaggering man. Exactly my type.

Everyone's type, right? This doesn't have to turn into a big thing.

I perch on the edge of the mattress and stare at my phone. I really don't know what's wrong with me tonight. I'm a very rational person normally. Steady as they go, that's me.

I can't believe I hung up on him twice.

I press the button to return his call, my hand not entirely steady. As soon as he answers, I blurt, "Hi, Eli, sorry I accidentally hung up on you." *Twice.*

"Insurance and registration," he orders.

"Uh, just a moment." In my rush to get my purse from the floor, I bang my hand so hard on the nightstand that the pain makes my other hand drop the phone on the floor. Again. I slap a hand over my eyes, mortified that I can't get through a simple conversation with the man. I drop to the floor and scoop the phone up. At least it landed on the rug both times.

I take a deep breath before attempting conversation. "Sorry." That's all I can manage to get out.

"Are you okay?"

I'm not so sure anymore.

2

"Just tired," I lie. I'm completely wired, buzzing with adrenaline.

"Okay, I only need the insurance. I'm so used to saying insurance and registration from pulling people over, it just popped out. Actually, I say *license* and registration. Never mind."

I laugh, and it comes out breathy. "Sorry about our little fender bender."

His voice turns stern. "More like a collision. My car is brand new. It'll never be the same."

I nearly say a ding to his car was bound to happen sooner or later but refrain. Maybe Eli never gets in fender benders. It's not my first. "I really am sorry. It certainly wasn't intentional." I flip through my wallet and realize I don't have the card. "My insurance card is in my car. I'll take a picture of it and send it to you."

Silence.

"Eli?"

"Uh, yeah, sure. Spaced for a minute there. I should have filed a police report on the accident, but it's not too late to file. I can do it tomorrow."

"But it was so minor."

"It's easier to have it for the insurance claim. If you

don't mind, I'll stop by tomorrow morning to take pictures of your car and file the report. I'm on duty in the afternoon."

"Isn't that a conflict of interest? Filing your own police report?"

"Okay, then I'll ask Chief Daniels to stop by tomorrow morning. He's on duty at eight a.m. Work for you?"

My bakery doesn't open until nine, but I'm up early to bake. "Sure."

"Good. Hopefully we can get this taken care of quickly. Then I'll be out of your hair."

I'm unexpectedly disappointed after all my ridiculous nervousness. I like the sound of his voice, the assurance in it. This is a man confident of his place in the world. "How do you like being a cop?"

"It's good. I like knowing I'm helping the community. It's not all traffic tickets and responding to wildlife calls." His voice sounds warmer now.

I settle back to sit in bed, leaning on my pillow against the headboard. "Wildlife calls?"

He chuckles. "Yeah, someone will call the station for suspicious noise around their property, afraid it's a robber. It's usually a raccoon or skunk. Probably deer too, based on how many calls I've responded to where there's no sign of a problem at all. The deer just wander off."

"So you never wanted to move away from Summerdale, where there could be more exciting crimes to investigate?"

"Summerdale is where it's at. Isn't that why you moved back home to open a bakery?"

"It was serendipity."

"Say what?"

"I was unhappy at work, and I told Sydney I wanted to open a bakery. I love baking, and it just seemed so fulfilling to bring warm tasty goodness to people. She told me Rainbow was retiring and closing the café. Serendipity. Just when I was ready to move on to the next thing, there it was. I didn't think too hard about it, just made the leap."

"Any regrets?"

"I miss the social scene in Brooklyn." *Single guys are at a much higher density there.*

"We have a social scene here too. You just have to look for it."

"Like what?"

"Barbecues, hanging by the lake, the bar at The Horseman Inn, you might've heard about it."

I laugh. I spend tons of time there because Sydney owns it. It's the main hangout for me, Sydney, Audrey, and Kayla (she's Sydney's soon-to-be sister-in-law). Harper too when she's in town.

He continues. "Or were you referring to the hookup scene? I'll admit there's not much of that here."

I flush hot. It's weird to hear Eli talking about hookups. He's Eli. "Yeah, well, you can always find that if you're motivated enough. There's apps, and we're free to leave town."

His voice takes on a husky tone. "You do that a lot? Use an app?"

My nerve endings tingle, alarming me. Just from his voice on the phone. *Really?*

I clear my throat. "I feel like we've gotten off track. I'll send my insurance. Get in touch when you hear about the estimate."

"Hey, no judgment. I was just curious. I never see you with anyone."

Do not engage. End this dangerous line of conversation.

"What about you?" I blurt. "Do you use an app for hookups?"

"I'm old school. Face-to-face. I meet people all the time, friend of a friend, hanging at a bar or club."

"You go to clubs?"

"Yes, ma'am. I like to dance, and women like a man unafraid to get out there."

My lips part in surprise. Eli's not the straight-laced guy I thought he was based on his profession. Of course, he was mischievous as a kid and downright bad as a teen. He used to steal cars before he finally got a clunker of his own. Sydney was afraid he was going to end up in jail. Now Eli issues orders to keep people in line. The ultimate irony. It's a wonder Chief Daniels hired him at all.

"Where do you go to dance?" I ask.

"Different clubs in SoNo." That's South Norwalk in Connecticut, about a half-hour drive southeast of here. "Occasionally I'll go to the Happy Endings bar in Clover Park, though it's not as much of a pickup scene there." Clover Park is also a half hour away, due east. Summerdale, New York, is near the Connecticut border.

"I didn't know they had dancing at Happy Endings." That's a restaurant and bar on Main Street in Clover Park. Way back before my parents' divorce, my family used to go there for Sunday brunch and then walk around the cute downtown just for a change of scenery. That was before everything went to hell when I was nine.

"Yeah, they expanded the bar in back to include a dance floor and billiards room. It turned out really nice."

I love dancing but refrain from asking to join him. First off, Sydney would kill me. Second, this is the same guy who used to steal our popcorn and jump out behind a corner when we went looking for him, tossing the popcorn all over us. He wore footed pajamas. Little Eli.

And now he's a swaggering alpha male, which I'm really trying not to think about. He did bring me roses before I went to college. Do I really know him at all?

"Still there?" he asks.

"Sorry. I got distracted." *Head spinning more like.*

"Alright, I'll let you go. I'll be in touch about the repair."

I say goodbye and hang up, running a hand through my hair, a little disoriented. I don't know this grown-up version of Eli, and the scary thing is, part of me wants to.

~

Eli

I head over to Murray's on Tuesday, which is the auto shop in town. They do repairs and minor bodywork. It's around noon, and Jenna's meeting me here. The appointment for the estimate worked out perfectly because Jenna's shop is closed on Tuesdays, and my work shift doesn't start until five. I figure we can get Jenna's car looked at too. She has a sizeable dent in her back bumper.

I step into an open garage bay. There's two bays, both with a car in them. I peek under an old white Toyota, where short legs in blue coveralls are sticking out. "Hey, Sloane."

She rolls out from under the car, her amber eyes striking against her dark hair and the smudges of grease on her forehead and cheek. "Eli, just give me a minute to seal this back up." She rolls back under the car. Sloane Murray was a year behind me in school and just recently moved back to town.

A few minutes later, I direct Sloane over to my Mustang. She winces, looking at the damage. "Such a shame for a brand-new beauty like this."

I stare at the front bumper, my voice somber. "I know."

She peers around the sides of the bumper and under it.

My eye catches on the red Honda Accord pulling into the lot. Jenna waves at me, and I lift a hand, telling myself to play it cool. Just because I used to have a thing for her and I haven't been able to get her out of my mind since she ruined my car doesn't mean anything's going to happen. I'm no longer that lovestruck teen in the throes of a killer unrequited crush.

I have experience.

I have options.

She pulls up next to my car and steps out.

I have a killer unrequited crush. Dammit. It wouldn't be so bad if she didn't know it, but she does, ever since I gave her those roses with the note I would do *anything* to take back. What the hell was I thinking making a hail-Mary pass the day she's leaving for college? My only excuse was that I was too young to think it through. Sixteen, pumped on testosterone, with years of built-up longing. I gave her my heart, and she patted me on the head and said, "Thanks, buddy." *Patted my head!* Like I was still a kid. Of course, she didn't know about the note when she patted me. I tucked it into the paper wrapper because I didn't want her to read it in front of me. Still, so damn embarrassing.

I'm surprised she hasn't mentioned it. Maybe she's embarrassed by it too. If that's the case, we can move on as if nothing ever happened. That would be ideal. Yeah, let's go with that. A man needs some dignity.

Her light blue blouse is unbuttoned just enough to display the curve of her cleavage. My mouth goes dry as my gaze trails to her narrow waist and the slight curve of her hips in tight white pants, ending at the curve of her shapely calves. Tiny white socks in white sneakers.

She elbows me in the ribs. "You're much less intimidating in the light of day."

"I intimidated you?" This is Jenna Larsen, sex goddess, confident woman.

"My car!" she barks in a deep-voiced impersonation of yours truly. She postures in front of me with her shoulders hitched up. "You'll pay for this!"

I shake my head, smiling. "I did not sound like that. Besides, you offered to pay. Hopefully, insurance will cover most of it, so there's just the deductible."

Her eyes linger on my lips before she turns abruptly to Sloane. *Interesting.* "How bad is the damage?"

"I'll have to order a new bumper," Sloane says. "Fortunately, the surrounding area is intact."

"What do you think of her back bumper?" I ask.

Jenna slaps my arm playfully. "Fresh."

I grin, enjoying this new flirty vibe. What was I so worried about? She probably never gave my note a second thought with all the excitement of leaving home for her new adventure in college.

Sloane shifts to inspect the Honda's back bumper. A moment later, she jams her hands on her hips. "I'm estimating a couple of thousand for Eli's work. Fifteen hundred for yours, Jenna. I looked up replacement bumper cost before you got here and, fortunately, there's not a lot else that needs to be done. Just some touchup work. I'll send the insurance companies a detailed estimate for both cars. Let's see how much they agree to cover, and I'll get back to you for the go-ahead."

"Fifteen hundred!" Jenna exclaims. "Forget that. I can live with a dent in my bumper."

"It's really not safe to drive a car with a damaged bumper," Sloane says. "You want it to protect you in case of another accident."

Jenna presses her lips together before turning to me. "How much is your deductible?"

"Thousand."

"Mine too. This is a very expensive fender bender. Plus my insurance will go up because it was my fault." She worries her lower lip, finally looking as upset as I am about the whole thing. Somehow it's not much consolation.

I step closer, wanting to make her feel better. "Let's grab some lunch, and we'll work out the details."

She nods. "Okay, sure, where?"

"The Horseman Inn is closest. Plus I happen to know the owner."

She smiles a little, her brows still knitted in concern. "Yeah, me too. I'll meet you there."

It's a date.

3

Jenna

This is *not* a date. I'm having lunch with Eli for a specific purpose. It's just that the air feels charged between us, and I've caught him checking me out a few times. Probably because I've been checking him out too. I never noticed how beautiful his hazel eyes were before. There's a thin light brown ring around the green with glints of gold throughout. His dark brown hair is trimmed short, emphasizing his masculine wide-set cheekbones and clean-shaven jaw. And I can't help but notice how his snug black T-shirt stretches across his broad chest and wide rounded shoulders. Bulging biceps, muscular forearms, big man hands. I can admit it. He grew up into a world-class hottie.

I glance guiltily around. Sydney's here somewhere, probably back in the kitchen at the moment, and I can't help but wonder what she'll say about the two of us having lunch together. It's completely innocent, but what if I can't hide the lust I'm battling?

I pick up a fry and dip it in ketchup. I usually just have a salad for lunch, so today I went for a hot lunch—warm roast beef sandwich and fries. It's heavenly. I was blessed with a high metabolism, so I can eat whatever I want. Good thing too because I always sample my newest baking creations. "So what did you have in mind?"

His hazel eyes are intent on mine. "What do you mean what did I have in mind?"

My face heats, which is odd. I hardly ever blush. Nothing fazes me. "You said we'd work out the details about the fender bender."

"Oh, yeah." He takes a sip of water. "I don't want you going broke over this. Just contribute whatever you can, and I'll cover the rest."

"Eli, that's not right."

"You could pay me in installments. Is that better?"

I let out a breath. He's being kind, much more than I expected after how angry he was before. The truth is, I'm on thin margins at my bakery, still paying off startup costs for the new equipment I had to buy. "No, this is my fault. I shouldn't have said anything about the cost. I'll take care of it."

Sydney pops up by my side, her light brown eyes darting between me and Eli. Her long auburn hair is up in a high ponytail. "Hello. What's going on here?"

I try for a neutral expression, careful not to look directly at Eli or her. "We were just working out the details on paying for our fender bender. It's expensive, and both of our cars have damaged bumpers."

Sydney gasps, grabbing my shoulder. "Are you blushing? I bet I know why. Did Eli confess when he was fifteen—"

Eli cuts her off. "Syd, you know what would be great?"

Sydney sends him a sly look. "What's that, little bro?"

"If you moved along," he says. "Jenna and I have a lot to discuss."

I study him, his expression is serious, his jaw set. No blushing. What happened when he was fifteen?

Sydney taps the side of her nose at him. "Got it. As you were." She leans down to my ear. "I just love embarrassing him. Big sister's privilege." She moves on to check on the next table, doing her manager thing.

I risk a look at Eli. What's so embarrassing from when he

was fifteen? Did it have to do with me? I was seventeen at the time and very involved in school activities and going out with my friends. I don't remember anything happening involving him.

He leans across the table and whispers, "She's so irritating, you can admit it. I won't tell her."

My lips curve up. "She used to say the same about you."

"True back then, but most younger brothers live for that stuff." His voice turns husky. "Do you find me irritating now, Jenna?"

I swallow hard. His eyes search mine. He wants to know if I find him appealing now. *Too damn much.*

I glance across the room, catching Sydney's eye. Her brows lift in question.

I turn back to Eli, trying not to look too interested. "What happened when you were fifteen?"

He leans back in his seat. "Nothing at all."

I lean across the table, keeping my voice low. "Then what was she implying? Did it have to do with me?"

He lifts one large shoulder in a careless shrug. "Who knows?" He goes back to eating his turkey sandwich.

There must've been something, but I drop it. I can always ask Sydney later. Still, I feel uneasy sitting here with him while Sydney hovers nearby. Like I'm doing something wrong.

I lean forward and whisper, "We probably should've gone somewhere else for lunch."

"Next time," he murmurs.

There's a promise in those words that brings a flush of heat to my entire body. Our gazes lock for a charged moment, and every nerve ending springs to life. I tear my gaze from his and take a long drink of iced tea. I remind myself why I'm here. I messed up his car, can't afford to fix his car or mine, and need to work something out. *This is not a date.*

"I'd like to pay you in installments," I say. "I'll write up a payment schedule and sign something to make it official. I'll pay interest too."

"That sounds good, minus the interest. So what made you leave computers for cupcakes?"

His voice is rich like chocolate—deep and warm—wrapping around me. I could listen to that voice all day long.

"Jenna?" He sounds amused.

I jolt out of my wayward thoughts. "Sorry. Uh, interest. Yes, I definitely need to pay that. It's the least I can do, considering the accident was my fault."

"No interest. Those are my terms. Now answer the question. I want to know about you."

I rub the side of my neck, my lashes fluttering down. "Thank you."

He tips my chin up with one finger, giving me a slow, sexy smile that melts my insides. "What made you trade computers for cupcakes?"

He really does want to get to know me, and I find I want to share.

"Well, after spending six years configuring hardware, software, and networks, all while responding to every tech crisis, I felt like my soul was dying. The only thing that made me happy was baking on the weekends. I took some night classes, learning more about pastry and baking, and started to realize this is all I want to do. I want to create delicious confections that make people happy."

He smiles, and it lights up his handsome face. "So making people happy makes you happy."

"It does. God knows, I never made people happy fixing networks. They expect it to work at all times, freak when it doesn't, and then when you fix it, they blame you for it breaking down in the first place. Cupcakes and brownies are much more forgiving."

"Do you have anything healthy on the menu?"

"Absolutely. My carrot cupcakes offer one-fourth of your daily serving of carrots."

He chuckles, his hazel eyes sparkling. "Maybe I'll stop by."

"You might also like my cider doughnuts."

He jabs a finger at me. "Don't even go there with a cop and doughnuts joke."

I laugh. "Sorry. It's just part of my seasonal menu."

We smile at each other for a moment before going back to lunch, eating in companionable silence. I relax. He's safe, in a way, because I've known him for so long, and I know he comes from a good family. I have to wonder why we haven't crossed paths since I moved home last summer.

When I finish my sandwich, I push my plate away, something bugging me enough to finally say it out loud. "You know, you haven't visited Summerdale Sweets once since I opened."

His eyes widen before he grabs his napkin and wipes his mouth. Finally, he says, "I should've stopped by to check it out."

I lean forward. "You should have. I was insulted that you didn't. Everyone else in your family did. Even grouchy Drew bought three boxes of cookies to share with his karate students."

He scoffs. "Right, you were insulted. You didn't even notice I existed until you backed into my car."

I gesture vaguely around us. "I saw you around town working. I didn't want to interrupt you on patrol." *And you looked too tempting in your uniform.*

"Maybe I didn't want to interrupt your baking."

"Come on. Just admit you were avoiding me."

He stiffens and looks at a point over my shoulder. "Why would I avoid you?"

I throw my hands up. "I have no idea."

He leans back in his seat, relaxing again. "I was busy catching troublemakers. Nothing personal."

It sure felt personal. I search his expression, but he's got a great poker face. I can't tell if he's lying. I don't know why it bugs me so much that he never stopped by. It just seemed like he was the only one in town who didn't, and it must be on purpose. "I never said or did anything to offend you, did I?"

"Nope. Nothing at all." He holds up a finger. "In fact, I

don't think you said more than 'get out' to me since I was thirteen."

I wince. "Only because it was girl time."

He inclines his head. "Anyway, enough rehashing old times."

Since I'd rather not dwell on what he used to be to me—Sydney's irritating little brother—I drop it. It really messes with my head to think of him like that while trying not to openly lust after him. "What's the worst crime you've encountered in Summerdale?"

He presses his lips together, trying for a grim expression, but his eyes are sparkling with good humor. "You don't want to know."

I lean forward. "Tell me."

"I regularly caught Rainbow sunbathing in the nude at the lake. I told her she had to cover up."

I laugh. "She was a true hippie." Rainbow was one of the original founders of Summerdale. A group of hippies in the sixties planned it as a kind of utopia. I bought her old café when she retired to Florida last year. She used to serve green drinks and salads with alfalfa sprouts. Even so, she was very supportive of my sweeter take on things.

"Are you happy here?" he asks.

I consider that. "I love my shop and being back with Sydney and Audrey. Kayla now too. She's a sweetheart." Kayla is engaged to his older brother Adam.

"But…"

I wipe my mouth with a napkin and push my plate away. "No one is happy about everything."

"Do you miss your old life in Brooklyn?"

"I miss the adventure of going out on a Saturday night with the potential to meet someone interesting."

"Interesting means hot."

I glance around, looking for Sydney. She must've went back into the kitchen or her office. "They need a brain too. I do have standards."

"So no hot idiots for Jenna Larsen, huh?"

I laugh. "Exactly."

"Head over to the Happy Endings bar on Saturday night. You might be surprised at who you meet." He winks.

My face flushes. He's coming on to me. Would it be so bad if I met up with him out of town? Yes. Because then I'd have to face him here in Summerdale, probably for years to come. And Sydney would find out.

"Or not," he says.

"I can't think of you that way."

His eyes are hot on mine, his voice low and husky. "I think you already do."

I lick my lips, and he watches the movement. Desire pools low in my belly. "I can't. You're a permanent fixture of a town I plan on staying in for the foreseeable future. That means potential future awkwardness if things don't work out and, in my experience, things never work out."

"It's just a drink, Jenna."

How can I explain I don't stick with anyone without revealing my damaged history? He doesn't know all the grisly details of my family, and I don't want him to see me that way. Not to mention Sydney wouldn't approve.

"Nothing personal," I say because it really isn't personal. I enjoyed our lunch. I just know when to cut ties—early before any real damage is done.

He studies me for a long moment.

"Looking mighty serious," Sydney sing-songs as she approaches. She stops at our table, looking back and forth between us. "Did you figure out the car thing?"

"About to," Eli says tightly.

Sydney salutes him and strides over to the bar.

He lifts his brows at me in question.

"Just friends, okay?"

He pulls out his wallet, tosses some bills on the table, and stands. "See ya around." He strides toward the door before I can reply.

"I'll be in touch!" I call after him. "With a check and paperwork."

He lifts his hand in acknowledgment before he walks out the door.

I stare at my plate. "Thanks for lunch," I say to no one.

Sydney plops down in his seat. "So-o-o, what's the deal?"

I sigh. "I worked out a payment plan to pay off the damage to his car."

"That was generous of him not to want it up front."

"Yeah, it was."

She pulls the bill out from her apron pocket, counts out the money he left, and pockets it. "He's a generous tipper too. Thank you, Eli."

"What were you teasing him about from when he was fifteen?"

She gestures me closer. "He'd kill me for saying this, but he asked me if you had a type back then. I thought he had a crush on you. It was so ridiculous to me at the time I didn't mention it. I mean, we were seniors, and he was a lowly sophomore. Anyway, I forgot about it until just now when I saw you having lunch together. I don't think I've ever seen the two of you together without me. Weird."

"Actually, it was kinda nice," I say softly, looking toward where he just left. "He's—"

"Don't even tell me you're thinking of making a move on my baby brother," she snaps.

My head whips back toward hers.

Her voice is fierce. "Not going to happen. I know you, Jenna, you *freak* at the idea of a lasting commitment, and you leave a trail of broken hearts everywhere you go. You hurt Eli, well, that's something I could never forgive."

I suck in air. I knew she wouldn't like the idea, but to hear her say it like that scares the crap out of me. I can't lose my best friend, the closest thing I have to a sister. "Okay, got it."

She gives my arm a squeeze. "Sorry, I know I can get a little over the top about Eli. Caleb too." She lifts her hand and curls her fingers. "The claws come out for my cubs. I'm like their second mom since our mom passed. They needed me."

"Sure, I know. Only the best for your little bros."

"Exactly."

I push down the hurt that I don't fit in that "best" category. Sydney knows my damage, and she wants her younger brothers to have only smiles and sunshine.

She continues in a conspiratorial tone. "Wyatt and I have been talking about setting Eli up with Wyatt's sister Brooke. They're the same age, and Brooke just wants a nice guy to settle down with." Wyatt's her husband, and they have a true partnership in everything.

I met Brooke at Sydney's wedding. She's pretty, nice, and smart. The absolute worst.

"Doesn't she live in New Jersey?" I ask. "Long-distance relationships never work out."

"She's an architect. There's buildings and houses around here." She smiles. "Wyatt's hoping to get all three of his sisters to settle here eventually. He got Kayla, though I think Adam had more to do with that than Wyatt. Too bad his sister Paige is too headstrong to match up with one of my brothers. She's more like Wyatt. What's wrong?"

I blink rapidly, willing myself to pull it together. "Nothing. Sounds like you and Wyatt are building a dynasty out here." *And I'm on the outside.* It's not like I even want a relationship. I'll never risk that kind of pain for myself, a guy, and definitely not on poor unsuspecting kids. I've always known I'm better off alone, though now that I'm twenty-nine, I sometimes feel this...longing. I haven't admitted this to anyone, but I think it might be nice to have a baby. Do the single-mom thing so a relationship wouldn't affect my kid.

She smiles widely. "A dynasty? Ha! Wouldn't that be cool? I'm the matriarch of course. You can be my right-hand woman, helping me keep order."

I swallow over the lump of emotion lodged in my throat. I'm well aware my friends are moving on to a new phase of life. I just never thought I would feel so very alone in the midst of the closest thing I have to a real family.

I look toward the door, where Eli just left. The man who had a crush on me finally asked me out, and I rejected him. Not only that, I dented his brand-new car. No wonder he walked out. He must hate me.

The words are out of my mouth before I can stop them. "Eli's a good guy. I feel awful."

"Why?"

I can't share that I turned him down. It'll bring up too many questions, and then she'll know I'm lusting for her brother. I can get over lust, I assure myself. It's good that I nipped this in the bud before anything got too complicated.

I let out a breath. "I don't know. Because of his car and because he's being so nice about it."

"What's wrong with him being nice about it?"

My eyes get hot. "Nothing." I shake my head. "I have to go."

I grab my purse and head toward the door with a quick bye over my shoulder.

"Jenna."

I wiggle my fingers in the air, unable to face her when my throat's tight, my eyes hot. It's just too much, being left behind while my friends move forward with their lives. And as crazy as it seems, I feel like I screwed up turning Eli down.

But what choice did I have?

I yank open the front door, get in my car, and make the short drive back to my apartment. I only survived my parents' divorce because of my girlfriends. I let them in close and no one else. Too risky. I was eleven when the dust finally settled between my parents after a two-year ordeal, where my sister and I were caught in a tug of war between them. They even fought over the dog, my beloved lab mix, Charlie, before giving him away because they couldn't agree on who got to keep him. My dog! I loved that dog. He was my only comfort at the time, licking my face and leaning against me with his warm furry body in his own form of a doggy hug. I still miss him.

My younger sister, Evie, and I had to go before a judge and decide who we wanted to live with. I chose Mom; Evie chose Dad. I tried to get Evie to stay with me, but she only wanted Dad. I haven't been close with her since.

That's why Sydney means so much to me. She was my

sister when my own sister abandoned me. Sometimes it feels like my entire family abandoned me.

And now even my honorary sisters are abandoning me for their own families.

I wipe my eyes. Some part of me doesn't believe I deserve love. I'm too damaged. It's a fact I've accepted, and I've never regretted pushing any guy away. Until today.

4

Eli

Friends. If that's what Jenna wants, we can be friends who ignore the attraction between us. Oh, yeah, I saw the lust in her eyes yesterday at lunch, the flush to her cheeks, the warmth in her voice as she leaned across the table. I know when someone wants me. So now we'll be friends, both knowing there's a *mutual* attraction.

I walk down Peaceable Lane, heading to her shop for a friendly visit, as I said I would. She noticed I was avoiding her, and she was pissed about it. Not one mention of my note. It seems the obvious embarrassing reason someone might want to preserve their dignity. Didn't it mean anything to her? Well, I'm not bringing it up this late in the game. I'm just going to right the wrong, make a quick visit to her shop, and then we can move past all that. As friends.

I slow my walk, taking in her shop. There's a painted red wooden sign over the front door that reads Summerdale Sweets in bold white letters, dark green awnings over picture windows, and two park benches right out front to encourage people to linger. It looks inviting. The shop's on the lower level of a white square building in the "downtown" area of Summerdale. If you could call a post office, small grocery store, The Horseman Inn, Jenna's shop, the library, and two churches at opposite ends of a long winding street a downtown. The streets are laid out like wavy spokes on a wheel radiating out from Lake Summerdale. The hippy founders worked around trees when making the streets, and they gave the streets groovy names: Peaceable Lane, Lovers' Lane, Sunset Lane, Harmony Lane, and Schoolhouse Lane. The road around the lake is Lakeshore Drive. Just on the edge of town is Route 15 leading out into the big bad world.

I open the door to Summerdale Sweets, and the bell above it jingles. It's Wednesday afternoon, and Jenna's busy with a couple of teenaged girls, so she doesn't notice me at first over their loud chatter trying to decide what kind of brownie to split. Jenna's dark green apron over a black turtleneck and black skinny jeans are a striking contrast to her blond hair and fair skin. *Beautiful.* An all-too-familiar lust rushes through my system.

She notices me, her green eyes widening. "Eli, this is a surprise."

"I thought I'd check out your place."

She nods and turns to the girls. "Salted caramel brownie is our bestseller. Can't go wrong."

The girls—a brunette and redhead—confer in a silent exchange of looks before turning back to her, saying in unison, "We'll take it." I recognize them now. Anna and Christina. Their families have been here for about three years now, ever since our regional high school was rated best in the state. I assist with security at the high school football games, which draw a large enthusiastic crowd, as well as visit the school regularly to discuss the dangers of drunk driving, staying off drugs, and also letting them know resources they can turn to for help, including me.

The girls pool their money to pay and turn to go.

"Hi, Officer Robinson," Anna, the brunette, says.

"Hi," Christina says, her gaze roaming from my green T-shirt to my jeans and sneakers. "You look, uh, *different* out of uniform." She shoots a look at Anna I can't interpret.

"Yup," I say, unsure if she just insulted me or not. Especially when they giggle on their way out of the shop.

Jenna calls out to me. "Grab a seat anywhere. I'll get your check and the paperwork I drew up to cover paying your deductible. Have you heard any news from the insurance company on how much they'll cover?"

"Not yet."

I glance over at the three small round tables at the front of the shop and head for the one in the center. The chairs are kinda small, white metal with a pink round cushion. I don't think Jenna had men in mind with these chairs.

As soon as she sits across from me, she gets right down to business, handing me a check for one hundred dollars. Then she hands me a paper that spells out paying in hundred-dollar installments once a month until her debt is paid down for the thousand-dollar deductible. She added five percent interest, which is high, and I said I didn't need that. She must not make much at this place if she can only afford a hundred dollars a month. If her bakery is failing, she'll probably leave town for a new job, which would suck. She's only been here a year. *Why did I avoid her for so long?* It seems stupid in retrospect. She's moved past my teenaged blunder, so I can too.

She hands me a pen. "You can make changes if you'd like. I was guessing on the interest rate."

"You didn't have to add interest. We go way back. Let's call me scaring years off your life as a kid popping out behind doors and corners as a fair trade."

She shakes her head, smiling. "You never scared me. I was onto you and never let my guard down."

"I seem to remember a few Jenna screams."

She waves that away. "For show to make you feel good. You put in a lot of time waiting quietly to pounce."

I lift a brow. "You were humoring me?"

She pats my head. "Poor little Eli, the truth comes out. You were never the terror you hoped."

I stiffen but manage to paste on a smile. The "little Eli" doesn't bother me nearly as much as the pat on the head.

Here's my heart, Jenna. Please accept these flowers with a secret love note.

Thanks, little Eli, pat, pat.

She never took me seriously, not then, not now. It was never just lust. I adored her.

It's way past time to move on. I clear my throat and take the pen from her, sign her paper, and hand it back to her.

"Why're you being so nice to me?" she asks.

I put on my neutral cop face. "I'm nice to everyone."

"But you seemed so angry before."

"I'm over it. It was an accident. Now it gets fixed and I move on."

She studies me for a moment before taking the pen and signing the paper.

I pocket her check. Part of me would like to walk out this door with my manly pride intact, and part of me wants nothing more than to soak her in. *Decisions, decisions…*

"You grew up into a good guy," she says.

I can stay a little longer. "Have to set the example when you wear the badge."

"It's more than that." She smiles and leans across the table. "You used to be so naughty."

I give her my sexiest smile and lower my voice to a husky tone. "I can be naughty when the occasion calls for it."

She blushes and straightens, rubbing the side of her neck. "I bet." She meets my eyes with a smile. "You're a flirt."

"Guilty."

Her lips curve up as she folds the signed paper, tucking it into her apron pocket.

Remind me again why we're just friends? She said it wasn't personal. Something about things not working out and potential awkwardness. So does that mean she never dates anyone in town in case she has to see them around? It's not like a lot of single guys come through here. What is her deal?

I glance around. Not the time or place to push her. *Nice and friendly, let her get comfortable with you.* "How's your bakery doing?"

She smiles brightly, her green eyes lighting up. "It's going well. I have regular customers." She stops smiling. "Oh. I see. You're wondering why I gave you such a small amount as payment, aren't you?"

"No, I figure you paid what you could. Don't worry about it."

She gestures toward the back of the shop. "I put everything I had into renovations and baking equipment last year. Rainbow hadn't updated the place since the sixties. It needed a lot of work. I also renovated the kitchen and bathroom upstairs in my apartment at the same time. So that was my savings; plus I borrowed some money. And now I have a mortgage and debt for the first time, which I'm not complaining about. This is my dream come true. I just don't have money for extras like a car accident."

I rub a hand over my clean-shaven jaw, considering letting her off the hook completely. There's that soft spot again. "Got it."

"Let me get you something on the house. You've never had one of my treats." She gestures to the glass case displaying cupcakes, brownies, bar treats, and cookies.

"I don't eat sugar."

She eyes me suspiciously. "Never? Not even on your birthday or Christmas? This is a momentous occasion—Eli Robinson visited my shop. In fact, I'll put up a plaque so visitors know. Why, I bet business increases twofold!"

"Smartass. I wouldn't mind a bottled water."

She rolls her eyes and walks toward the counter. I follow her over, my gaze falling on the sweet curve of her ass.

She glances over her shoulder, catching me looking. I jerk my head up. *Busted.*

Her voice sounds breathy. "Why don't you come back here with me, and we'll share a small plate of something. I really should be behind the counter in case someone comes in."

Nothing could keep me away.

She slices a salted caramel brownie in half and puts half on a small white plate for me, gesturing toward the stool next to the counter.

"You can have the stool," I say. "I don't mind standing."

She grabs a bottled water and napkin for me, handing them over before taking the seat. "Eat."

I take a bite into fudgy decadence, my eyes widening. "This is the best brownie I've ever had."

She preens, tossing her hair back. "It's my bestseller." She takes a bite of her brownie. "Now you're officially Team Jenna."

I'm saved from admitting I've always been Team Jenna by the bell jingling over the front door.

Joan Ellis walks in, the grandmother who raised Harper, one of Sydney's best friends. Harper called her General Joan behind her back because she barked out orders military style. I know Mrs. Ellis because she was a third-grade teacher at my elementary school. I never had her, but my friends who did complained endlessly about their homework load. She's got to be in her eighties by now. Her hair is white and short, her brown eyes sharp. She dresses as though she's still going to work every day. Today she has a white scarf tied around her neck, a peach-colored blouse, and black pants. Her black shoes are thick soled, her only concession to her bad hip.

"Hi, Mrs. Ellis," Jenna says, suddenly standing stiff and straight. *The General is in!* "Can I help you?"

"Bah. I'm eighty-eight years old, fit as a fiddle. You think I got this way eating sweets? Sugar is the devil."

I chuckle. "See? I'm not the only one who avoids sugar."

Mrs. Ellis turns her sharp gaze on me. "Eli Robinson, you're looking fit. So if you're not here for sugar, why are you here?"

I flush guiltily as though my lust is showing. It's unnerving the way she seems to see right through a person. Now I know why Sydney always said they were all scared of her. "Thought I'd check out the place everyone's always raving about."

She gives me a knowing look before turning to Jenna. "He'd be good for you, Jenna. Solid and stable, a real man. They're not so easy to find nowadays, so when you do, make sure you do something about it. Has he asked you on a date yet?"

My jaw gapes, and I close it with a snap.

Jenna flushes bright red, gesturing toward me, her mouth open but nothing coming out. Finally she puts her hands on her hips, looks to the ceiling, and lets out a breath. "Mrs. Ellis, surely that's not the reason you stopped by today."

Mrs. Ellis gives me a pointed look. "Looks like it's time for you to step up here. She's clearly overcome at the thought. A good sign."

I grin. "I'm on it, Mrs. Ellis."

She rubs her hands together. "Excellent. Jenna's good people."

Jenna's eyes are huge, staring at me. I wink at her behind Mrs. Ellis's back, figuring she'll look relieved, but instead she searches my expression. *Does she want me to ask her out again?*

Mrs. Ellis gets down to business. "I'm here about the Fall Harvest Festival. I wasn't satisfied with the way the meeting ended last night." The Fall Harvest Festival takes place the last Saturday of September on a large piece of preserved land next to the Presbyterian church.

Mrs. Ellis pauses.

And keeps pausing.

Finally, Jenna bites and says, "Why weren't you satisfied?"

"Because we still don't have enough for the kids. It's all about the beer tent and concessions."

They get into a detailed discussion over the festival. Jenna's polite and respectful, even when Mrs. Ellis declares she has the solution to bring people together—square dancing.

Jenna shoots me a horrified look. I grimace.

Mrs. Ellis goes on cheerfully. "The kids always enjoyed square dancing in gym class. They'd come back to the classroom sweaty and red faced. Good clean fun."

"More like embarrassed," Jenna says under her breath.

Mandatory boy-girl square dancing in gym class was definitely embarrassing at that age. Boys didn't want to link arms with a *girl*. Barf. And girls thought the boys had cooties. They were always screaming about them.

"What's that? Speak up!" Mrs. Ellis barks at Jenna.

"I don't think square dancing is the answer," Jenna says evenly.

Mrs. Ellis arches a brow and looks at me. "Do you agree?"

"I do. It's not what kids are into nowadays."

"Well, we need something!" Mrs. Ellis exclaims. "I swear, kids don't know how to have fun anymore. It's all about pressing buttons and staring at screens."

Jenna looks thoughtful. "I'm sure we can come up with something, though it's only a little over two weeks away. We can't get too ambitious."

"A dance-athon," Mrs. Ellis says with a note of finality. "That's it. We'll do it in the big red barn from five p.m. to midnight so the dancers don't get too tired out. Kids, adults, everyone together." The big red barn is the long-standing home of our very own Standing O theater company.

"Hmm," Jenna says.

Mrs. Ellis continues enthusiastically. "We'll ask the dancers to get sponsors and use the money to fund next year's festival and make it even bigger. People can wander over to the barn to watch."

"We'd have to ask the Standing O if it was okay," Jenna says. "And what about music? We'd need to hire a DJ or get a live band."

"I'll leave that part to you," Mrs. Ellis says. "I'm just the idea lady. You young people have the energy to make stuff happen. Good talk." She points to the case. "I'll take one of those chocolate chip cookies to go. You know, just in case Harper visits soon."

Jenna gives her a knowing look. "You'll need a few more, then. She's got a husband and baby now."

Mrs. Ellis sighs dramatically. "Might as well make it a dozen. My son-in-law Garrett is a big man." Her face softens. "Caroline is two months old and smiling now." She opens her purse and pulls out a small wallet-size photo of the baby.

"She's beautiful," Jenna says with a touch of longing. Her eyes go soft. *Interesting.*

Mrs. Ellis shows me the picture too. Caroline is a chubby baby with a pink bow on her tiny wisp of light brown hair.

"Happy-looking baby," I say, unsure of the appropriate thing to say.

Mrs. Ellis pulls the picture close, smiling at it for a long moment. "I wasn't sure I'd live long enough to be a great-grandmother. Harper sure took her time finding a real man."

I smile. That's what she called me too—a real man. Quite a compliment from the General.

Jenna hands over a bakery box of cookies. "You'll live forever, Mrs. Ellis. Enjoy. Tell Harper to stop by next time she's in town."

Mrs. Ellis pulls a crisp twenty-dollar bill from her wallet and hands it over. "I'll call her when I get home to let her know cookies are waiting."

She gets her change and makes her way out the door, limping a bit with her bad hip.

After she leaves, Jenna says, "She's going to order Harper home all the way from Brooklyn so the cookies don't go to waste. I know how she operates." She takes her seat again and takes a bite of brownie, looking up at me under her lashes.

I'm drawn in all over again. No woman has ever compared to her.

I finish the brownie in two more bites and set the plate by the sink. "Amazing."

"I can tell you liked it because you wolfed it down. Can I tempt you for more?"

I step closer, my gaze dropping to her pink luscious lips. "I can easily be tempted."

"Eli." Her voice sounds breathy.

I close the distance, tucking a lock of hair behind her ear. Her green eyes are wide, staring into mine; her lips part.

I lean down and brush a kiss against her cheek before speaking softly close to her ear. "I'll see you again soon."

I straighten and meet her eyes. She puts a hand to her cheek that I just kissed, blinking up at me.

I tilt my head. "Okay there, beautiful?"

She recovers herself, standing and tidying up behind the counter. "Yes, sure, I need to get back to work. Very busy. Lots to do."

"Bye, Jenna."

She stills, studying me for a moment before saying softly, "Don't be a stranger."

I smile, turn, and walk out the door. *Friends. Ha.*

5

Jenna

I'm with my girls on Thursday for ladies' night at The Horseman Inn. Sydney had to go check on something in the kitchen, but she'll be back. We call ladies' night our Thursday Night Wine Club. It started out as a book club—Audrey's idea, our favorite bookworm. Anyway, we spent way more time drinking wine and chatting than we did talking about the book, so Sydney dubbed it Thursday Night Wine Club. Audrey was miffed at first, but now she has a real book club at the library on Tuesday nights for people who are much more serious about discussing great literature.

I'm nursing a dry martini, and Audrey's sipping her favorite pinot grigio. I swear she tries to look like a librarian. I mean, she is one, but that doesn't mean she has to dress like one, right? She's wearing a light blue blouse with a Peter Pan collar, a navy cardigan, and gray trousers with loafers. At least her long black hair is down instead of up in a bun held together with pencils. Yes, she actually does her hair like that at work sometimes, and then she forgets about it and goes out like that at night too.

The fact that we're both sitting in the longtime-owned Robinson family restaurant, trying not to notice two Robinson guys we've known our entire lives, isn't lost on me. Eli and

Drew are at a corner table at the far end of the bar, watching the Yankees on the TV. Somehow things changed. A new perspective in my case? A miscalculation in Audrey's case? Sydney and I believe Audrey got up the nerve to tell Drew, Sydney's oldest brother, her feelings for him sometime around Christmas last year, and it didn't go the way she hoped. She's been cool to him ever since. Despite the fact that we're as close as sisters, Audrey refuses to discuss it.

Drew's a badass loner dude who Audrey has loved since she was six. Crush at first sight. He was eleven. I honestly never thought her crush would last this long. In my opinion, it's become a problem, preventing her from moving on. She's my age, twenty-nine, and says she's ready for marriage and kids. For a while there, she was making a valiant effort to use eLoveMatch to find her Mr. Right. Lots of first dates with guys she never saw again. As far as I know, she's never had a date with Drew.

I'm busy not looking at Eli in a white button-down shirt and jeans. Casually hot. We had a moment at my shop yesterday. A *heart-pounding, he's about to kiss me* moment that I couldn't have stopped if I wanted to. The pull was too strong to resist. He kissed my cheek, a tender gesture of affection that made my skin warm and tingly and left me wanting more.

Audrey elbows me. "Why do you keep looking at Eli?"

I avert my gaze. "I'm not."

"Yes, you are. Did something happen between you two?"

I sip my martini, feigning nonchalance. "We met up a couple of times about the fender bender. He was—" *Wonderful. Tender. Sexy.* "—gracious about it."

Her blue eyes widen. "Eli was gracious? The same guy who terrorized us at sleepovers?"

I find myself smiling. "He was a terror, wasn't he? Now look at him, such an upstanding member of the community." I catch his eye, and he gives me a slow sexy smile. Warmth rushes through me, my body humming in anticipation.

Audrey leans against my shoulder. "Well, now, wasn't that flirty? He *is* a police officer now, and Sydney says he takes good care of his new pit bull mix, Lucy. They've had some doggie playdates." She straightens, looking thoughtful. "Okay, I'm on board. A man with his life in order, who loves his dog, means he's one of the good guys now. Does Sydney know you're into him?"

"Don't say a word to her," I whisper fiercely. "She warned me off him."

Her brows shoot up in surprise. "Why?"

"Because she wants better for him." I press my lips tightly together to keep them from quivering. The truth cuts deep.

"I'm sure that's not true."

"It is! Just drop it!"

"Okay, okay, sorry." Audrey gives me a sympathetic look. "For what it's worth, I think it would be great for you and—"

"Shh."

She lowers her voice. "If anyone can handle a reformed bad boy, it's you."

I tuck my hair behind my ears. "Thank you, I think. He was never really bad."

"Jenna, he stole cars. That's bad."

"But he gave them back. It's more like he borrowed them from people in the community. Sort of like that program they have in the city, where you take a car and drop it off at a certain location for the next person."

"Uh-huh. And let's not forget how he stole our snacks, dropped popcorn over our heads, and scared the crap out of us, sneaking around corners and popping out of closets. I swear I slept with one eye open at every slumber party for ten years."

I shake my head. "You were seriously scared of a boy two years younger than us?"

She narrows her eyes. "He was capable of evil."

I glance at Eli, looking so chill watching the game. "Yeah, all right. So instead you develop a mad crush on the quiet one who turned into a finely tuned assassin."

"He is not an assassin!" she exclaims, and then turns bright red, realizing she's given away the fact that she's still hung up on Drew. She's denied it fiercely, but she can't fool me.

"Sure, okay."

Audrey is still fired up, defending her love. "He was an Army Ranger and left the military with honors. Drew would never intentionally scare anyone or do any of that stuff Eli did."

"Finish your wine. You're going to need it." I'm tired of her pining for a clueless guy. She needs to either get with him or get over him. "Hey, Drew!" I call. "Got a minute?"

Audrey grabs my arm in a death grip. "What are you doing?"

"I just want to talk to him."

"No. Be cool."

Drew gets out of his chair, his eyes glued to Audrey.

"Too late," I whisper. "Are you afraid to talk to your life-long crush?"

Drew ambles over to us in his silent but deadly way. His brown hair is freshly cut—short on the sides, long on top—his jaw scruffy as usual. His dark gaze lands on Audrey for a long moment, but she refuses to make eye contact, staring at his chest. "What's up?"

I elbow Audrey.

She sends me a death glare, tosses back her wine, and meets his eyes, her cheeks flushed pink. "Nothing much," she chirps. "Just wondering if you would be at the thing on Saturday with your demo. Not next Saturday, three Saturdays from now. If you weren't busy."

"If by Saturday thing you mean the Fall Harvest Festival for our karate demo, then yes."

She waves him away. "That's all we needed to know, thanks and have a good night."

He shifts closer to Audrey, his voice lowering. "I get the feeling you're avoiding me lately."

"Nope," she says to his chest. "Not at all."

He glances at me, and I face front as though I'm not listening. Just sipping my martini here, taking in the delightful sounds of ladies' night. There's a group of women knitting to my left, talking and laughing. I almost wish I could ask them to lower the volume to help with my eavesdropping.

Drew's voice is gruff. "It's been since last New Year's Eve. Nine months now. That's enough time to get over whatever you need to get over."

I can't resist peeking.

Audrey's face flushes red with anger, her eyes flashing. "There's nothing to get over. Nothing whatsoever, and there never will be." She turns away and lifts her hand to the bartender, Betsy, gesturing for another glass of wine.

Drew stands there for a moment, staring at her, but she refuses to look at him. "Right." He turns and walks stiffly back to his table.

I wait until Audrey has her wine. "What's the deal with him? Come on, Aud, you can tell me. You know I'm on your side."

She stares at the bar, her brow furrowed. "Just drop it. Seriously." She takes a healthy swallow of wine and turns to me with a smile plastered on her face that's not fooling me for a minute. "I'm not dating anyone until I know they're Mr. Right. So if that means I'm single for the rest of my days, so be it."

"So you don't want him anymore? You're really moving on?"

She traces a circle on the bar top, her eyes downcast. "I want Mr. Right."

"What if there is no Mr. Right? What if there's only a Mr. Almost Right and needs some training?"

She laughs a little. "Like a puppy."

I smile. "Exactly like that."

Her lips form a flat line, her expression grimly determined. "I'd prefer if another woman trained him, dumped him, and then he came to me fully ready to be my Mr. Right."

I sigh. "That's the dream, isn't it?"

Sydney pokes her head between us. "Hello, ladies, what're we discussing?"

I turn to her. "Well-trained men."

She beams. "Oh, man, did I luck out in that area. Wyatt

grew up with three sisters. Not only is he savvy to PMS, he always puts the toilet seat down."

We laugh.

"Jenna and I were talking about much better training than that," Audrey says. "The kind of guy that positively radiates Mr. Right. Like you just know right away."

Sydney shakes her head. "Didn't happen that way for me. Seriously, unless Right is his last name, I don't think that exists."

I hitch a thumb toward Audrey. "It's what she's waiting for."

Sydney opens her mouth and then closes it again, probably refraining from mentioning Drew. We both want Audrey to move on. It's just been too long. "I hope you find it, Aud." Sydney throws an arm around her in a quick hug. "You should get back out there."

Audrey groans.

I take pity on Audrey, wrapping an arm around her shoulders. "Does it get any better than this? Drinks with my girls on a crisp fall night. I love this time of year."

Sydney leans across Audrey to look at me. "Okay, now you're scaring me. What happened to jaded Jenna?"

"Can't I just enjoy the fall?"

She studies me for a moment. "You hooked up with someone, didn't you?" She turns to Audrey. "She has that freshly fucked look on her face, right?"

Audrey turns to me, her brows shooting up, a question in her eyes. She knows who it could be. She turns to Sydney. "Nope. That's not her freshly fucked look. That's her *happy with my business* look."

Sydney and I both laugh. It's always funny to hear prim librarian Audrey use the F word. She's not really prim, she just looks the part. A lot.

Audrey sighs. "Must you always laugh when I speak frankly? I'm not a prude."

"Frankly," Sydney and I echo before cracking up.

"What's all this noise?" a masculine voice demands.

My gaze collides with Eli's, his hazel eyes sparkling with

amusement even as he keeps a stern expression on his face. A shimmer of excitement radiates through my entire body, making every nerve ending tingle; even my stomach flutters. It's only Eli I've ever reacted to like this. "Is there a problem, officer?"

He leans in. "I might have to arrest you for disorderly conduct."

I offer him my wrists. "If you must."

He holds my wrists manacled in one hand in a firm grip. My pulse races, a shock of sensation rippling up my arms. "Tempting."

My breath hitches as I imagine the intimacy of being cuffed by Eli. Naked. What would it feel like, the weight of his big body, the heat of his skin. What would he taste like?

He trails a warm finger lightly over the inside of my wrist before releasing his hold. One corner of his mouth lifts. *Could he feel my pulse pounding through the delicate skin there?*

He inclines his head at Sydney and Audrey. "Ladies, as you were."

He swaggers back to the other end of the bar, taking his seat with Drew.

Someone snaps their fingers in front of my face. I turn to Sydney, belatedly realizing my misstep. I was so happy to see him that I forgot to act cool and casual. "Yes?"

"Hello! What the hell was that?"

My gut does a slow roll. I face front, trying for a neutral expression as I take a sip of martini. "Nothing."

"That wasn't nothing," she snaps. "You were coming on to Eli."

"I wasn't." I feel myself flush. "We were just joking around."

Audrey pipes up. "I'd say he was coming on to her. She can't help it if he flirts with her. You don't want her to be rude to him, do you?"

I appreciate Audrey's support, but I'm not sure that's any better. Sydney looks angry.

"Did something happen?" Sydney asks.

"No, nothing. We're friends."

Audrey looks between us anxiously. She's the peacemaker of our little group.

Sydney eyes me. "Then what's he doing here on ladies' night?"

I wipe my sweaty palms on my jeans. It's true we don't usually see him here on ladies' night unless he's stopping by for a quick pop-in on his shift as a cop. "I don't know. It's his family's restaurant. Isn't he here regularly?"

"Yeah, on Saturdays twice a month to play guitar," she says drily. "Do me a favor and don't encourage him. I don't want him to get hurt."

"Got it," I manage over the tightness in my throat. It pains me that Sydney sees me as the villain in this. I'm not a terrible person. I down the rest of my martini, my heart aching, my body going numb.

My gaze wanders back to Eli. He winks. My face flushes with heat, and for the first time I ask myself a question that makes me queasy and excited at the same time—

What would happen if I took a huge leap of faith and followed my heart?

But then that possibility vanishes as Sydney's stool scrapes the floor in her rush to get out of her seat. "I need to have a talk with Eli."

Eli

My sister approaches with a grim look of determination in her eyes. She grabs a chair from a nearby table and plops herself down at our small table, putting herself squarely between me and Drew, but it's me she's focused on. "Don't get involved with Jenna."

Drew's head swivels toward her in surprise and then turns back to the game. He doesn't want to get in the middle of our sister going mama bear in one of her overprotective gestures. She's only like this with me and Caleb because we're younger than she is. She means well, which is the only reason I tolerate it.

"Syd, it's none of your business," I say.

"It is my business when it comes to you. She's only going to break your heart. And I say that as her best friend. You don't know her like I do. She's great at friendship, terrible at relationships."

I let out a breath, reaching for patience. Sydney did a lot for me as a kid, but I'm not a kid anymore. "Since Mom died, you've looked out for me, and I appreciate that."

She smiles and gives my arm a squeeze. "Of course. That's what family's for."

I gesture toward Drew, the oldest in our family. "Just like Drew looked out for you when we were kids. But we're all adults now."

"I know that," she says. "Doesn't mean I don't look out for you and Caleb."

"Drew, did you get involved in Sydney's love life in her best interest?"

He grimaces. "No."

I lift a palm. "See?"

"That's different," Sydney says. "Drew didn't know any of the guys I dated well enough to warn me off. I'm telling you, Jenna is not for you."

"You say that like you know who's for me."

"I know what you deserve. Someone without a lot of baggage who can love you unconditionally. Someone who's looking to settle down and hopefully, down the line, get married and have a family. You want that, don't you?"

Drew tunes back into our conversation, seeming curious about my answer.

"Yeah," I admit. "No rush, but yeah."

Sydney leans closer. "That's not Jenna. She's never wanted that kind of life." She straightens. "Actually, Wyatt and I thought you might be a good match for—"

I cut her off. "I don't need help finding someone. I already found her."

Her voice takes on a soft motherly tone like when we were kids. "Eli, I'm trying to save you a lot of pain and heartache here."

Drew slowly shakes his head. "Syd, he needs to learn the hard way."

I scowl. "So you think it'll end badly too?"

He lifts one shoulder in a careless shrug. "I've got no opinion either way. My point is, you can only learn by experience, and no amount of well-intentioned advice will have any effect."

Sydney turns to me. "Even if you ask her out, she won't go for it. I already told her I'd never forgive her if she hurt you."

I glance over at Jenna, who quickly looks away, her shoulders slumping. She probably knows Sydney's talking about her. This is getting out of hand.

I give Sydney my sternest cop look. "Don't get in the middle of this."

"I already am. She's my best friend; you're my little bro. I have to look out for your best interests. Who else is going to do that?" She means because our parents have passed.

I blow out a breath and shoot Drew an exasperated look. He inclines his head slightly, an imploring look in his eyes. He wants me to keep the peace with Sydney.

Fine, but I'm doing it my way. "Okay, Syd, I'll think about what you said. Thanks for having my back."

She tears up and grabs me in a fierce hug, practically choking me. She turns to Drew for the same, but he shoves her head instead.

She gives me a watery smile and goes back to her friends.

As soon as she's out of hearing range, Drew whispers, "You're going behind her back, aren't you?"

I take a pull on my beer. "Is there any other way?"

He inclines his head. "But—" he lifts a finger "—if this thing with Jenna does go someplace, you have to tell Syd. Don't leave her in the dark for long, or it'll be a mess. I don't like a mess in our family."

"Agreed."

6

The next day before I start my late shift at work, I text Jenna a simple question that somehow feels like tiptoeing through a minefield. *Dinner on Saturday night?*

She responds immediately, probably already home from work.

Jenna: *I'm not available.*

Me: *You mean you're seeing someone?*

Jenna: *No.*

Me: *Is Syd the problem?*

Jenna: *She's right, you know. I'm not what you're looking for.*

I clench my jaw and type quickly. *How do you know that if we never spend time together?*

There's a long pause. Just when I'm thinking she's not going to answer, another text pops up.

Jenna: *I'm going to be really busy working this holiday weekend anyway. Labor Day weekend is nuts around here.*

This is true, and I'll be working a lot too. Not only does everyone in town celebrate the last long weekend of summer, but a lot of out-of-towners rent lakehouses and have parties. Still, I'm not giving up so easily. I just need to dial it back, give her an option that feels safe.

I text back: *Next Saturday after that. Come to The Horseman Inn and watch me play guitar. Casual friendly outing with no witnesses. Syd and Wyatt will be at a fundraiser in the city that night.*

I wait as three dots appear. She's about to answer, and I realize I'm holding my breath. The dots disappear.

I let out a breath. Dammit. I shove the phone in my pocket and get ready for work.

On Saturday night I'm back at The Horseman Inn, playing acoustic guitar. I haven't seen Jenna in a week, but she's never far from my thoughts. I can't help but think if she was really into me, she wouldn't let Sydney hold her back. Though I understand her not wanting to lose Sydney's friendship. I don't have anything to lose in that regard. Sydney will stick by me no matter how much I screw up. She was my staunchest defender as a wayward teen and helped smooth the way to keep any serious charges from being held against me.

But Sydney's not here tonight. Neither is Jenna.

I change my sheet music to a new song, a ballad by Bob Dylan, and begin to play. Locals like the mellow background music, and it relaxes me. It's also my way of contributing to the family business. The Horseman has been in my family for four generations. I practically grew up here since my dad owned the place when I was a kid. There's a good crowd at the bar tonight. Betsy's handling it like a pro.

After I finish the song, I look around. A few customers clap politely, which I acknowledge with a nod and a smile. And then *she* walks in, alone, heading straight toward me in a red dress with a black leather jacket thrown over it. High-heeled black leather boots. My heart thumps double time. She flashes a smile and takes a seat at the corner table diagonally across from me.

I tuck my guitar in its case and walk over to her. "Hey, you made it."

She shoos me away. "I want to hear you play."

"Haven't you heard it before? I'm sure you must've been here on a Saturday night once or twice."

A slow smile spreads across her beautiful face. "I was always distracted by my friends. Tonight I'm going to really listen."

I lean close, breathing in her floral scent. "Any requests?"

She looks up at me, her green eyes soft, almost vulnerable looking. "Whatever you usually do."

I put my hand over hers and give it a squeeze. "I'm glad you're here."

Pink tinges her cheeks. "It's nothing." She glances around. "Don't make a big deal."

I head back to my chair to play some more from my repertoire. Usually I play from seven to ten. It's now eight. Will she stay the whole time?

I play a ballad, occasionally glancing at her to see what she thinks. Her gaze is warm, her body swaying in time to the music.

She's into me.

~

Jenna

I was ridiculously nervous about showing up here tonight. I went back and forth on it so many times, and now that I'm here, I'm so glad I went through with it. I'm just one of a crowd in the back room, and Syd's in the city tonight. It's perfectly okay to listen to him play. Is there anything hotter than an alpha male in touch with his sensitive side? Eli plays guitar like he's coaxing the gentlest, most intimate notes from it, music that reaches into my soul. No words, just notes tumbling over each other, building to a crescendo, and then fading away.

I'm enthralled, wrapped in a soft cocoon that contains only the music, me, and Eli.

"Jenna, what're you doing here all by yourself?" Audrey asks, startling me. I hadn't checked in with Audrey about coming here.

"What're *you* doing here?" I ask.

She gestures toward the dining room behind me. "Just finished dinner with my parents." I wave over at Mr. and Mrs. Fox.

She gives me a sly look, leaning her head toward Eli. "So-o-o?"

"I was curious. You know, about all the fuss over the Saturday night entertainment."

She sits down at my table and whispers, "You're really into him."

"Shh." I glance over at Eli, but his head is bent over his guitar. No indication that he heard.

"It's not a big deal," I say. "I just wanted to hear him play."

"Right."

We both glance over at him, and he gives me a slow sexy smile. I flush, my stomach fluttering. There it is again—butterflies in my stomach. I used to think women made that up.

Audrey leans in, whispering, "I'd say it's mutual. Are you actually going to give him a chance?"

I watch Eli's fingers stroke the guitar, and I desperately want those hands on me. All of him on me. I can't believe how much I want him. And I'm not so sure it's just regular lust anymore. I really like him. "I don't know."

"You don't know? Well, this is major progress. That's the first time I've ever heard you even *consider* that it might go somewhere with a guy." She grabs my hand. "Sweetie, you deserve love. You can't let your parents' screwup affect your future."

The reminder makes adrenaline spike through me. I'm playing a dangerous game here. "I should go."

She sighs. "You don't have to go. I'll stop bugging you about this. Have a good time tonight." She walks back to her parents, and they head out the door.

I sigh. What am I doing here on a Saturday night listening like a fangirl to Eli play guitar? What did I think would happen?

I shouldn't have come. This is only going to blow up in my face.

The music stops. My head jerks up, my heart kicking up speed as his gaze eats me up.

"This one's for you," Eli murmurs.

My breath stutters out.

He starts to play, and I recognize it, Aerosmith's "I Don't Want to Miss a Thing." He's not singing, but I can hear the lyrics in my head. It's about treasuring every moment. My breath hitches. I can't leave now.

I'm barely aware of the crowd surrounding us. Warmth fills me up, like I'm floating along with the music.

And when the song ends, I clap, my eyes stinging, my throat nearly closed with emotion.

He gives me a tender smile.

This time my heart flutters for the first time ever. I'm scared of all I'm feeling, yet I can't seem to leave.

And when Eli finishes for the night, he puts his guitar away, walks over, and takes my hand, pulling me up with him. "What did you think?"

My voice sounds breathy. "I liked it. A lot." But I mean him.

He smiles, his hazel eyes lighting up. "I have the early shift tomorrow, so I need to go. You want to walk me out, or did you want to stay here a little longer?"

"I only came to hear you play. I'll go too."

He gestures for me to go ahead of him, and I walk through the restaurant, feeling self-conscious. Will the waitstaff report that I left with Eli? I'm just walking him out. Guilt weighs heavily on my shoulders.

Once outside, I gesture toward my car parked in the back corner of the lot closer to the road. "Well, that's me over there."

He walks with me to my car, carrying his guitar case. "Thanks for coming tonight."

I'm overly conscious of his presence by my side, his sure confident stride, the five-o'clock shadow on his jaw. "Sure, it was fun."

We get to my car, and the area lights up from the motion-sensor light perched in the tree above us. I freeze, standing in the spotlight with him. Can the people inside the restaurant see us?

"Well, goodnight." I quickly turn away and unlock my car.

"Hey," he says gently.

I turn back to face him, steeling myself against him. I have to resist temptation. And not just because of Sydney. I'm not cut out for relationships, and he's not someone I could ever be with casually. Too complicated. Even knowing all this, I don't move away. Instead I stare at him, taking in the fine arch of his brow, the thick lashes framing his eyes, the sharp angle of his shadowed jaw.

He smiles, and my butterflies take flight. He's got the most beautiful genuinely warm smile. It lights up his face. It lights me up. "I want to take you out, somewhere away from judging eyes, if you know who I mean."

I do. Of course I do. Panic flashes through me, making my heart pound. Still I don't move away.

He takes my hand, turning it and lifting my wrist to his mouth. A jolt of raw desire goes through me at the touch of his lips. I'm sure he felt my frantic pulse.

When am I ever going to find another man like this—alpha and tender? He does something to me, makes me feel sensations I've never had before, emotions I've never let myself feel before. *Dangerous*. My mouth is dry. I can't seem to find the words to push him away. He's still holding my wrist, and I like it.

One corner of his mouth lifts as he sets my hand back by my side. "Tempted?"

"Yes," I whisper.

"That's all I need to know. Goodnight, Jenna." He opens my car door for me, and I slip inside on shaky legs.

What did I just agree to?

I'm back at work early as usual on Monday morning, baking up fresh muffins, brownies, and layered bars. I'll get to the cookies later. Audrey put in a large order of my bestselling salted caramel brownies for her book club, so I had to get here extra early to ensure I had enough for her order and my usual inventory.

Usually I'm a little groggy in the morning, but I'm filled with energy. Almost jubilant. I don't know what's come over me. I've only had one cup of coffee. I have a sneaking suspicion why I'm so jubilant, but I don't want to think too hard about that. It makes me feel jumpy that I sort of agreed to see Eli away from judging eyes. I haven't heard from him since then. Maybe he was too busy yesterday to text me about it. Or maybe he's having second thoughts. I deflate, my jubilance taking a dive.

The timer dings. I pull a tray of brownies out of the oven and set them to cool. That catchy song from Aerosmith has been stuck in my head ever since he played it for me. No one's ever dedicated a song to me before. Another sweet gesture. He was also so kind about working out our little fender bender problem, even though I know he was upset about his new Mustang. I shake my head at my dreaminess and, since I'm alone, I play my work playlist of upbeat songs. It helps to have a good beat.

I get into a rhythm, the delicious smells of cinnamon, sugar, and chocolate wrapping around me. Even as much as I bake, that never gets old. The scents, the textures, the taste. I simply love it.

Two hours later, I take a seat and put my feet up. We open in an hour. I eat a fresh pumpkin muffin and do a mental checklist of what I need to do before I open. My mind wanders back to the man who's never far from my thoughts.

Is Audrey right that I'm letting my parents' stupid mistakes ruin my future happiness? God, isn't it enough that it ruined my childhood?

I put my feet on the ground and sit up straight. Am I really going to do this? Attempt a relationship? My heart pounds in my ears, and I go cold all over, nausea roiling in my stomach. I sit back and take a few breaths. I can't. The fallout with Syd. The bone-crushing disappointment when it goes up in flames.

I close my eyes and force myself to focus on work—my inventory, my orders for the week, recipes to consider for the upcoming holiday season.

Two hours later, I'm going through my inventory spreadsheet in between a few customers, desperately trying to stay focused. As long as I stay focused on what I can control, I'm fine. I'm not thinking of anything but Summerdale Sweets. Truth is, I haven't thought much about anything else for more than a year, ever since I opened last summer. I haven't even taken a day off. I have a part-time assistant who bakes early for me a few days a week, but the rest is all me. I never worked harder than when I worked for myself.

The bell jingles, and I close my laptop, standing to greet my customer. My eyes widen in surprise. It's Audrey and Eli. They're not usually together. Eli looks rugged and manly in a blue plaid flannel shirt, jeans, and hiking boots, like he's about to go hiking on this beautiful fall day. My gaze returns to Audrey, smiling widely. An inkling of unease goes through me.

I'm almost afraid to ask. "What's going on?"

Audrey marches up to me. "You're officially off duty. Apron, please."

"What!"

Audrey smiles. "You're getting a small vacation."

My brows furrow in confusion. "I have to work."

Eli crooks his finger at me. I walk around the counter and join him. He's not smiling. In fact, he looks almost menacing. His eyes gleam, his jaw set.

My breath hitches. "Eli, what's going on?"

He moves so fast I only catch a glimpse of shiny silver before I'm handcuffed. "I'm kidnapping you."

7

"What the hell?" I yell.

Audrey claps. "He's stealing you away like when he used to steal cars. Remember you called it borrowing? Now he's borrowing you! He promised to bring you back."

I glare at her and turn back to Eli. "I can't just leave. I'm the only one here."

He unties the strings of my apron and takes it off me, handing it to Audrey. "You did agree to let me take you out, away from judging eyes."

"I said I was tempted!"

He smiles. "Of course you are. Consider this a surprise road trip if it makes you feel better. You were surprised, and I planned a road trip."

"Oh, he's good," Audrey says.

He gives Audrey a roguish grin. "How do you think I made it out of so many scrapes without a mark on me?"

I lift my cuffed wrists. "I think kidnapping is more accurate."

He gets serious, pulling his shoulders back, in full cop mode. "You're under arrest for a two-day trip with yours truly, during which you will peep at fall leaves and various other things not to be mentioned in front of Audrey."

Audrey giggles.

Alarm shoots through me. *Two days away just us?*

I look wildly between the two of them. "I can't leave my shop!"

Audrey puts her hands on my shoulders, her eyes intent on mine. "I'm covering for you today, and you're closed on Tuesdays. Go. You deserve a break." She lifts my handcuffed hands. "Not like you can work with these on."

I turn to Eli, still in shock and not a small amount of worry about the outcome of spending so much time together. "I can't believe you're kidnapping me."

"Audrey said it was okay."

"*Audrey* said—" That's as far as I get before he upends me over his shoulder.

The breath whooshes from my lungs. No guy has ever attempted to carry me like this. I'm too tall for that. I try to hold onto my mad. What kind of guy kidnaps you? What kind of friend helps him do that behind your back?

Eli's already moving toward the door.

I focus on Audrey. "I'm so getting my revenge on you, Aud! You won't know where or when, but it's coming!"

She wiggles her fingers at me. "Have fun!"

And then I'm out the door, the sun poking through brilliant leaves just starting to sport yellow, orange, and red colors. We must be heading north if we're going on a leaf-peeping trip. I did *not* agree to this. I'm sure Sydney's going to find out if we're both out of town for two days. The man is crazy!

Eli sets me down by his Mustang. "Hope you don't mind I brought along my favorite female for the trip." He hitches a thumb to the back seat, where a light brown pit bull with white fur on top of her muzzle sits with her head hanging out the window. "Jenna, meet Lucy."

I'm not even his favorite female. And *I'm* tied up! Not the dog! *Grr…*

"Lucy isn't constrained like I am," I point out.

"Lucy leaps into my arms whenever I see her. You don't." He opens the car door, puts a hand on my head, and tucks me into the front seat like a criminal. I comfort myself with the fact that he didn't go so far as to handcuff me and shove me into his police car. What would people think? I'd never get any business again. The criminal brownie maker. They'd probably suspect I'd been sneaking pot into my recipes or something like that.

A moment later, he gets in the driver's side, reaches over, and puts my seatbelt on for me. Then he starts the car and takes off.

I lean my head back on the headrest, my mind bouncing along to what all this means. Obviously the man wants to spend time with me, and he'll go to great lengths to do it. And he made it easy for me to spend time alone with him. No waffling, no overthinking it, just kidnapped with my friend's blessing. My stomach flutters. Stupid butterflies.

I'm still mad. He didn't give me a choice, and as a business owner, I need to plan for time off. Not that I ever do. Ohh, that's why Audrey made a big order of my bestselling brownies for her book club. She wanted to make sure I had enough inventory for my time off. She is so thoughtful. No, wait, I'm mad at her too. She should've told me what he was up to. Or was it her idea?

"Whose idea was this kidnapping?" I ask.

"I guess I'd have to say it was yours. You did offer to let me cuff you at the bar a couple of weeks ago—"

"What! I did not."

"Oh, yes, you did. I said I might have to arrest you for disorderly conduct, and then you said, and I quote, 'If you must.' If baking brownies at five a.m. isn't disorderly conduct, well, then, I don't know what is. And let's not forget that only two days ago, you said you were tempted to go out with me, far away from judging eyes. I connected the dots, and here we are—handcuffed road trip. No judging eyes, just Lucy's adoring ones. Right, Lucy?"

"There's no such thing as a handcuffed road trip!"

"Lucy adores you already. Just look at her."

I shift to the back seat toward Lucy. She looks ecstatic to have my attention and leans forward to sniff me and then licks my chin.

I sit back in my seat. That's the great thing about dogs—they love everyone. *I just met you and I love you!*

I glance over at him looking pleased with himself. "You could've just asked me on a date like a normal person."

"Could I, or would you have been so worried about judging eyes that you turn me down despite the fact that you're into me?"

Dammit. I am into him, and I probably would've tried to resist for reasons that don't seem to matter so much now that the two of us are speeding along out of town. I look out the window, trying to hang onto my mad. It's wrong to kidnap someone. And handcuff them too!

I turn to him. "I'm not going to leap out of a moving vehicle. You can unlock my cuffs."

"I will."

I hold up my cuffs.

"In five hours. Once you're safely locked in our room. Or maybe I'll handcuff you to the bedpost. Think about it, beautiful. You, at my mercy."

My mind conjures that so perfectly I throb. *No. Stop. This is crazy.* I am *not* turned on by Eli doing the wrong thing. What if there was no one to cover for me at work? I can't afford to lose an entire day's worth of sales. Audrey smiling like a loon flashes through my mind. *Crazy lady.* She'll take care of my shop like it was her own.

He glances at me. "On a scale of one to ten, ten being kick-my-shin furious, how mad are you about being kidnapped?"

"Take my handcuffs off and see," I say sweetly.

He slides a sideways look at me. "I'm guessing ten. I probably should've tied your ankles together too."

"Don't get any ideas. So I guess I'm just supposed to wear the same clothes, never brush my—"

"Audrey took care of it. Bag's in the trunk."

My jaw drops. She has my spare key in case of emergency but still. "When did this happen?"

"This morning when you were at work. You're welcome."

I purse my lips. "Where are we going?"

"A lodge in the White Mountains of New Hampshire.

They take dogs, and we have a first-floor suite with a patio so Lucy can hang there if she wants. It's good leaf-peeping time up there too. Not peak time, where we have to fight the crowds, but enough to look colorful."

I want to be pissed and hammer home that what he did is wrong, but it actually sounds fantastic. I haven't had a real day off in forever. Even when my shop's closed on Tuesdays, I always end up doing laundry, running errands, cooking ahead for the week, bills, etc. All that boring adult crap. I never just chill.

He stops at a red light and gives me a stern look. "Don't expect sex on this trip."

My brows shoot up in surprise.

The light turns green, and he hits the accelerator. We're cruising along again while I sit there stunned. The man kidnaps me and gets us a room but doesn't want sex. And he even teased me about handcuffing me to the bedpost. I have to know.

"What kind of kinky game are you playing?"

He barks out a laugh.

"Are we sharing a bedroom?" He really is crazy if he thinks sex is not happening in that scenario.

"It's a two-bedroom suite. One room for me and Lucy to share, and one for you."

He'd rather sleep with his dog than me? Well, she is *his favorite female.* "You're kidding me."

"Nope."

"And what will we be doing on this surprise road trip where I'm handcuffed and you sleep with your dog?"

He grins. "We'll be hiking, apple picking, and eating ice cream. Your basic nightmare scenario."

A laugh escapes. "I can't believe you planned all this."

"It wasn't hard, and it gives me a chance to get to know you better."

I gulp, my heart thundering. "Someone could get hurt. And Sydney wants you to be with Brooke. She made it clear she wants me to leave you the hell alone. She knows how damaged I am."

"Brooke, Wyatt's sister?"

"Yeah."

"Why in the world would you think I'd just blindly be with someone my sister wants me to be with? She has no say in who I spend time with."

I stare at him. "Didn't you hear the part about someone getting hurt? That's what Sydney's so worried about, and, honestly, so am I."

He's quiet for a moment. "Listen, give me these two days, and then I'll leave you alone for good."

I blink. "Really? Just two days?"

"That's right."

I fidget in my seat, trying to wrap my mind around this. For some reason, I thought we were dealing with something much bigger here. The big R. Relationship. I don't know why I thought that. I guess there were some unexpected feelings on my part—really warm feelings—but he doesn't feel the same way. I should be relieved. It's just a secret casual thing. Not quite a fling since he said no sex. More like a secret getaway.

"What if Sydney finds out?" I ask.

"Audrey swore this would be a private venture." He grins. "Wouldn't look good if the future chief of police was a known kidnapper, and Syd is probably too busy with Wyatt to notice what we're doing on a Monday."

"And Tuesday."

"And Tuesday, yes. I never see her early in the week, do you?"

"No, not usually."

"Then what Sydney doesn't know won't hurt her."

He can't be so sure about Sydney. She could find out and be pissed I went behind her back, but it's not like I had a choice. I let out a breath of exasperation. I was handcuffed by a clueless alpha who didn't think through all the consequences.

I glance at him. He looks so relaxed behind the wheel. I can't fully relax until I'm sure he understands the gravity of the situation he's put me in. "Sydney told me she'll never forgive me if I hurt you."

"Do you plan to hurt me?"

"No, but I don't think she'd approve of—"

"Two days. That's it. If she finds out and gets upset, I'll deal with her."

"Sydney and I are like sisters. I want to be old ladies together, slugging back gin and cheating at cards."

He chuckles. "Is that you at the nursing home?"

"It sounds silly, but it's true. She's my people."

"That doesn't mean you keep out all the men people, does it? She's married now. If she can make room in her life for a man in between the gin and cards, then why can't you?"

"I'm never getting married."

"Okay."

"No, I mean it."

"I know you do. Relax. You're just being kidnapped on a two-day forced vacation, where you won't be getting any of my sweet loving. Enjoy."

I laugh a little.

It's only two days.

He stops at a red light, fishes a small key out of his pocket, and unlocks my handcuffs, tossing them in the cup holder. I rub my wrists, and he lifts them to his mouth, his hazel eyes intent on mine before placing a gentle kiss on the inside of each one. Heat flashes through my system, my pulse thrumming through my veins. It nearly feels romantic.

He glances at the light, still red, turns back to me, and wraps his hand around the back of my neck, pulling me close for a kiss. A jolt goes through me on contact. The graze of his warm lips on mine only makes me want more. A perfect first kiss.

He pulls back enough to look into my eyes. "I don't expect much, Jenna. Just a chance to get to know each other a little better."

My lips part in surprise. That doesn't sound as terrifying as I first thought. In fact, it sounds very doable. Two days of getting to know each other a tiny bit more. I must admit his expectations are set reassuringly low.

The light changes, and he drives on, taking the turn onto the highway.

I'm quiet as we drive, watching the beautiful scenery as we head farther north toward the foothills of the Appalachian mountains, the trees in blazing colors among stands of evergreens. The blue sky is dotted with wispy cirrus clouds, light and easy like things with Eli.

I relax for the first time in a long time. I'm going on vacation with a sexy man, who understands the need for discretion and clear boundaries. I don't think it gets any better than that. Add this to the list of things I've never done with a guy. Never went away together, never been kidnapped, and never had sex taken off the table. Hmm…

"Is kissing allowed?" I ask.

He winks. "Only if you ask nicely."

8

Eli

So far, so good. Jenna and I just settled in at the lodge—a large two-story log building—after a brief stop for lunch and a short hike by a waterfall on the way up. It's afternoon now, and the property around the lodge is filled with hiking trails through woodlands with a bubbling stream. Lucy is dashing around the suite, happy to be out of the car. We have a living room with a small galley kitchen, and two bedrooms on either side with their own bathrooms. There's only a few other couples here, according to the front desk clerk. Most of the place is empty. Not surprising for a Monday when it's not yet peak foliage time.

"This is so nice," Jenna says, looking out the glass patio doors to our view of rolling hills and woodlands. It's a beautiful day I get to share with a beautiful woman. I had originally thought of this as an extended first date, but after hearing all her worries, I realized I can't think too far ahead. Two days. A test of sorts. When it's just us, is there something worth pursuing despite what she considers her damage and the possible fallout with Sydney? I don't want her to lose that important friendship either. I'm hopeful about us, but a lot depends on how things go between us here, isolated in the mountains of New Hampshire. No pressure.

I come up behind her and wrap my arms around her. "I'm glad you like it."

She glances at me over her shoulder. "I thought we weren't having sex."

"Last time I checked, hugging someone fully clothed isn't sex."

"It's a preamble."

"Can't I just be affectionate?"

She turns in my arms, her arms wrapping around my middle. "Where did the lust go? Or was that just me?"

My lips curve up. "Oh, it's there, trust me."

She runs her fingers through the hair at the nape of my neck. "Maybe we could do other things."

I pull away, already too tempted. "Nope. I'm getting Lucy's leash, and we're going to explore the property."

"And after?"

"We're going to play poker while you spill all your secrets to me."

"Strip poker?" she asks hopefully.

I groan. "You're killing me here."

"I think it would be okay," she says softly.

I turn away, grabbing Lucy's leash. This is how it has to be. I know that on a gut level. I want to build something here, a foundation.

I call Lucy, and she barrels straight toward me, leaping into my arms. I laugh as she licks my face.

Jenna walks over, smiling. "This dog loves you like crazy."

"She's done that from day one when I got her from the vet, Dr. Russo. She was so grateful to be adopted." I set her down and snap her leash on. "Ready?" I ask Jenna.

She's still smiling at Lucy, only now her eyes are watery. "Yeah, I'm ready." She grabs her coat, and we head out through the patio doors.

"Fall's my favorite season," she says. "I love the cool temperatures, the leaves, all the delicious baking with apples, pumpkin, and cinnamon."

"I like it too. Mostly because it's a quieter time at work

once summer vacation's over. And the weather's not bad. Spring's my favorite though."

"Baseball season," she says.

"Exactly."

"Yanks had a good season." And then she surprises me, talking enthusiastically about the lineup and how she knows next season they'll go all the way. Most women aren't so excited about baseball. This is looking very promising. A woman who loves the Yankees as much as I do.

"We should see a game together," I say.

"I'd love that." She sobers. "I mean, we could probably get a group together or something."

"What's the weirdest thing you like to do?" I ask, trying to lighten the mood. I can't have her running scared. Building trust takes time, and I've only got her for the next thirty-six hours.

She shakes her head. "I'm not admitting that to you."

"Why not? I won't judge."

She bites back a smile. "Yes, you will."

"Nope. I'm sure I've seen and heard much worse around town."

"Like what?"

Lucy yanks at the leash, enticed by a squirrel. "Heel," I order, keeping her close to my side. She yanks once more and then looks up at me, her eyes begging me to let her get to her prey. "That's a heel," I say, feeding her a treat from my pocket.

Jenna looks at me expectantly. Oh, right. All the crazy stuff that goes on in Summerdale.

"I can only tell you stuff that was in the police blotter," I say.

"They still publish that? I thought the newspaper shut down."

"They've got one person, Mrs. Shire's daughter, who runs the whole thing and publishes it online."

"Huh. Is it still called the *Summerdale Sheet*?"

I guide Lucy closer to the stream, walking alongside the bubbling water. "Sure is."

"I've been missing out. I'm going to look that up. Give me a few news tidbits in the meantime."

"There's so many. I told you about Rainbow sunbathing nude in public, then there was the kid who secretly kept a squirrel as a pet, and then it got stuck inside the sofa. Hmm, what else? Mr. Needles crashed his car into his garage and claimed it was from a hurricane. Actually, that last one wasn't public. Keep that to yourself. He was hoping for insurance money, and I talked him out of committing fraud."

She smiles up at me. "You're good with people."

"Takes all kinds. Wouldn't it be boring if we were all the same?"

"I guess."

I take her hand, and it feels like the most natural thing in the world. "So what's your weird thing you like to do?"

"You can't tell anyone this ever. It would destroy my reputation as Summerdale's premiere baker."

I fake gasp. "What could it be? Do you pass off frozen pie as homemade?"

"Never!"

"Your cookies come from a tube?"

"No, no, no. Everything is authentic and made from scratch from the freshest ingredients."

"Then what? The secret ingredient is lard?"

She laughs. "No, only organic butter in my recipes. Okay, maybe my thing isn't so bad after all." She pauses and looks around, but there's no one here, just us, the squirrels gathering acorns, and one happy dog. "I like to eat frozen Twinkies dipped in milk."

I widen my eyes in mock horror. "No. Twinkies are the opposite of a fresh-baked good. They're cake shot full of so many preservatives they could outlive humanity."

She laughs. "Not that bad. I dip them in milk because the cake crumbles away and then there's just frozen cream. It's such a mess, but it's so good. And then I drink the milk with all the crumbs at the bottom."

"Blech. This I gotta see."

"It's not pretty. I've been eating them that way since I was a teenager, and even though I make really good homemade stuff, sometimes you just gotta have your frozen Twinkie in milk."

"I hear that. It's like me and my kale smoothies."

She eyes my chest and then my shoulder. "You drink kale smoothies?"

"Nah, that's Caleb. I was trying to come up with something as gross as your frozen Twinkie disintegrating in milk. I stick to food I can chew. Real food."

She bumps my hip playfully. "So tell me your weird thing you like to do."

I squeeze her hand. "I like to kidnap beautiful women named Jenna Larsen and not have sex with them."

"That is weird!"

We crack up.

~

Jenna

There's no nightlife here, which means after dinner in the lodge dining room, we go back to our suite. We had this amazing maple whiskey cider at dinner—I even got the recipe—so I'm thinking inhibitions are nice and low for the rest of our evening. Eli unlocks the door and holds it for me to go in first. Lucy barrels toward me, and I leap back.

"Lucy, sit," Eli commands.

She halts, looking unsure.

"Sit," he repeats.

She sits, her tail wagging hard. He pets her, and I move forward into the room, giving her a scratch behind the ears. She leans against my leg for a moment before trotting over to Eli, who's closing the curtains by the patio.

He crouches down and pets her before looking up at me. "I probably should train her to stop leaping into my arms when I come home. She almost did it with you, and she could knock you off balance."

That implies he expects me to be around his house enough to make training Lucy properly a priority.

"But it's just two days," I blurt.

"She still needs to be trained properly for other people." He pets her with both hands, rubbing behind her ears. "But it's so damn fun, isn't it, Lucy girl?" She wags her tail so hard, her entire back end wags. He stands. "I'm going to take her out for a quick walk, and then we'll play poker. Unless there's something else you'd like to do."

I glance toward the bedroom automatically and turn back to him. "Poker's fine."

His smile is slow and sure, his eyes knowing. "Cool. See you in a bit." He gets Lucy's leash and leads her out through the patio door.

I wander into my room and figure I might as well get ready for bed. What else is there to do? I grab my toiletry bag and head into the bathroom. I'll be minty fresh if we kiss, which could lead to more. That's only natural. No one could blame me for hooking up with him in a kidnapped overnight situation. Actually, no one would ever know what happened here besides Lucy, and she's not talking. The thought is liberating. At the same time, I know I need to be careful not to get too close. I already like him too much. I can't risk a deep attachment that gets ripped away.

Lucy's great too. I'm glad he brought her. I should get a dog. I just never went there after losing my dog as a kid to my parents' divorce. God, I even deny myself the company of a dog because of what they did. I have to stop punishing myself.

I'm punishing myself.

The thought makes me suddenly unsteady, and I grip the bathroom counter, staring at my pale reflection in the mirror. I never thought about it that way. Punishment for something I logically know isn't my fault, but some part of me—some deep down angry little-girl part—believes it is.

I splash water on my face. That's it. I'm getting a dog. Not the kind I had growing up. Something completely different. Maybe I'll get a pit bull like Lucy, and then they could play together. My heart races at the thought. A future with Eli and Lucy in my life.

Two days. That's all this is. Eli is not thinking like that. Don't be foolish.

Tomorrow I go home, back to my real life with my friends, my shop, and my cozy apartment. It'll be like this trip never happened. Except I find myself wanting to hang onto every moment with both hands. To have memories to look back on during lonely times.

I finish up in the bathroom and go to my black wheeled suitcase for my pajamas. Audrey didn't pack any lingerie for me. It's my usual *girls' night in* outfit of a navy Yankees T-shirt with matching plaid flannel pants. Guess Audrey wants me to focus on getting to know Eli, or maybe she knew he was a big Yankees fan and hoped it would entice him. Sex is easy; sharing intimacies is hard.

The only people who know my deep dark self are my closest friends. I've never shared anything like that with a guy. Mostly because nothing with a guy ever lasts long. It's not that I always choose the wrong guy, it's that after accidentally breaking hearts, I've learned to tell guys up front I only want casual. That way no one gets hurt. Most guys are relieved. With Eli, it was reversed. He told me how it would be after *kidnapping* me. I find myself smiling. I still can't believe he did that.

I walk out to the living room and take a seat on a small maroon floral sofa. There's a TV on the wall across from me. I guess we could always watch TV if we run out of things to say.

Eli arrives a short while later. Lucy bounds toward me, and I tell her to sit so she doesn't leap at me. She does, and I pet her. She pants happily. What a good dog.

Eli slowly removes his jacket, checking me out. "Those pajamas are *hot*. I don't think Audrey could've picked a better outfit."

I laugh. "Right. I'm sure the flannel pants really do it for you."

"You're a Yankees fan. That does it for me. Score one for Audrey."

I shake my head, smiling. "Ridiculous."

"Hold on." He goes into his room and returns with a deck of cards. "Here, shuffle these while I get changed."

"Okay." I shuffle a few times, my mind wandering to how tonight will go. Will he grill me for all my secrets? I've never had a slumber party with a guy before.

A few minutes later, Lucy leaps to her feet and rushes forward to Eli.

He commands her to sit. My mouth gapes. He's wearing a gray T-shirt and the exact same plaid Yankees sleep pants as me. He gives his pants' leg a tug. "Looks like we're a matching pair."

I groan. "Too weird."

He sits next to me, puts an arm around my shoulders, and gives me a squeeze. I flush hot, but he doesn't do anything more, just grabs the cards and deals them. He holds his cards close to his chest. "How're your cards?"

I scoot back. "Terrible." I've got a great hand, but I can't let him know. That's like poker rule *numero uno.*

One corner of his mouth lifts. "I'm glad you have a bad poker face. That means you're honest to a fault."

"And you're not honest?"

"I am, but I can be completely expressionless if needed. See?"

He looks completely blank. It's his cop face when he's looking into a situation—professional, calm, and neutral. "You know, I thought for sure you'd pull me over for speeding at some point."

"You speed but not as much as some people." He smiles, his hazel eyes dancing with amusement. "I once had to give General Joan a ticket for driving too slow. She was holding up a huge line of traffic."

I laugh. "I can totally picture that. All right, let's play."

~

We played three rounds—I won one; he won two. We laughed a lot and talked the whole time. It helps that we have a shared history because it was fun to catch up on old times from each other's very different perspectives, him being male and two years younger. That was a big difference when we were kids. There's a comfort level here I've never had with another guy.

"You want to watch a movie?" he asks.

"Sure."

He hands me the remote. "Lady's choice."

"Oh really? Most guys would be afraid I'd pick something too girly."

"You're wearing Yankees pajamas. I'm not worried."

I flip through the guide and pick out one of my favorite movies. It's about a group of male strippers, and the choreography is amazing. Yeah, that's why I like it—the *choreography*.

He grabs the remote. "Nope, you forfeit for choosing wrong."

I lunge for the remote, and he holds it just over my head. I try again and end up half on top of him, and I still can't reach it. The heat of his chest penetrates my shirt, and I look down at him. His eyes burn into mine.

My breath stutters out. "You really should let me choose since I was the one who was kidnapped."

"Yes, but you chose wrong."

"There is no wrong. I picked a wonderful movie."

"For women."

I'm about to protest when his hand cups the back of my neck, his eyes going half-mast.

"Ask me nicely," he murmurs.

9

"Kiss me, please," I whisper.

His lips meet mine in a soft brush and then again. I melt against him, desire spearing through me. *Oh, yes, more of this, please.*

Suddenly it's over. He lifts me off him, aims the remote at the TV, and turns it off. "Goodnight."

"Eli."

He's standing a few feet away. "I'll send Lucy in to wake you bright and early. We've got apple picking and a hike before the drive home."

Normally I'd be tired by now since I get up at five a.m., but I'm wired with energy. Apparently one kiss from Eli is like a jolt of caffeine.

"Don't go," I say. "We can watch something else we both agree on." *And kiss some more.*

He stares at my mouth. "I don't think that's such a good idea."

"But I'm not tired." *I'm lusty.*

He throws his hands up. "The things a kidnapper has to do. Okay, you sit on the sofa, I'll sit on the floor across from you, and we'll talk."

I try to hide my disappointment. "Talk about what?"

"About the many adventures of Jenna Larsen."

"There haven't been that many adventures."

He grabs a large purple velvet throw pillow from the sofa, tosses it on the floor, and sits with his legs crisscrossed on top of it. Lucy joins him, resting her head in his lap. "Talk. Start with what your life was like in Brooklyn. No judgment, and it doesn't leave this room."

I look away, nervous, but at the same time exhilarated at the freedom of sharing as much as I want without judgment. I hug the other purple velvet throw pillow to my chest and decide to test the waters. "At my old job, I had this complete a-hole boss. We fought like cats and dogs until one night we screwed on the conference room table after hours."

"Liar. Complete honesty or I'm out."

I suck in air. I can't believe he saw through my test subject so easily. Complete honesty, huh? Then I want to know about him.

"Have you ever been in love?" I ask.

He stills.

"Come on, complete honesty."

He studies me for a moment before finally admitting, "I once loved a girl named Beatrice."

"Beatrice," I echo. "Isn't that an old-lady name?"

"She was named for her grandmother. Anyway, Beatrice and I met at a club, and we stuck together for a good six months and a not-so-good three months after that. I ended it. She was not happy, to put it mildly. She refused to give me back the stuff I left at her place, and when she finally did, it was nothing but a box of ashes."

"Oh, wow, she burned your stuff."

"Yup, including my favorite shirt."

"Not a Yankees jersey, was it?"

"No-o-o. That would've been unforgivable. Just a button-down shirt I wore to clubs a lot. It was the perfect shade of green to bring out the green in my hazel eyes. At least that's what she used to say."

I set the pillow on the floor, stretch out on my side, and prop up on one elbow. "Were you devastated over it ending?"

"For a while, but I recovered. Your turn. And don't keep asking me questions to get out of sharing."

I roll to my back and stare at the ceiling. Then I get up and dim the light so it's not in my eyes. I flop down again. "I thought I was in love once. It was in high school. We went out a few times, always in a group, but I guess I got the idea in my head that we were at the same depth of feeling. Turned out he was really into someone else, and I was more of a pal he fooled around with. I was heartbroken, which sounds stupid because I was just a kid, you know? Seventeen. It happens. But I guess it turned me off relationships for a while."

Until I had one in college that I messed up. And another one after that too. I've learned my lesson, I swear!

He looks at me expectantly.

I hate admitting I'm incapable of being close to a guy, so instead I give him part of the truth. "I decided it wasn't worth the pain of having feelings that weren't returned."

"Understandable. Shortsighted but understandable."

We talk for hours. Not just about our histories, but also our dreams for the future. He plans to be chief of police soon, which I knew, but I also discovered he's good friends with the vet in town and wants to help him raise money for a shelter right in Summerdale. Eli is amazing. A man with surprising depth who cares about the community, including animals.

We're sitting together on the sofa now with a throw blanket over both of our laps. I got chilly at one point, and he brought me the blanket. Of course I offered to share. Now it's super cozy with our combined body heat. Lucy is on the pillow on the floor that Eli abandoned, curled up tight and sleeping.

I'm getting tired, but I don't want to say goodnight and end this wonderful time with him. "Do you have any dirty secrets?"

He nudges my shoulder with his. "You mean like your disgusting frozen Twinkie habit?"

I gasp in mock outrage. "What happened to no judgment?

And it's not disgusting. It's delicious. Don't knock it until you've tried it."

He takes my hand in a warm grip, lacing our fingers together on top of the red fleece blanket. His fingers are long and tapered, covering my smaller ones. "You're right. No judgment over what you're into."

I feel so close to him I want to climb into his lap, bury my face in his neck, and breathe him in. Taste him. Touch him.

His deep voice jolts me from my lusty daydream. "I do have one secret."

I give him my full attention, already smiling in anticipation. "What?"

He releases my hand, tucking a lock of hair behind my ear, his finger trailing lightly down the side of my neck. A shiver goes through me. "You were my teen fantasy girl."

I meet his eyes, my voice breathy. "Sydney said she thought you had a crush on me when you were fifteen."

He studies me for a long moment before admitting, "It was a little longer than that."

"Oh."

He faces front, probably embarrassed he shared.

I try to make him feel better. "Well, you were so young, I guess that's only natural. Like the way Audrey worshipped Drew, even though he was older and never seemed to notice her." I clamp my mouth shut because I was the older one, and it sounds like I never noticed him, but of course I did. "You brought me flowers the day I left for college. That was a nice gesture. It brightened an otherwise chaotic bittersweet day."

"Nice gesture," he echoes.

"Yeah, it was nice that you stopped by to say bye and bring me a little present."

His jaw clenches. "That's what you thought it was? Just a little present?"

I blink a few times, confused. "Uh, it was a great present. Who doesn't like getting roses? I wanted to take them with me to my new dorm, but—"

"So the note meant nothing to you?"

"What note?"

He stares at me.

"Eli, what note?"

He speaks slowly and carefully. "The note with the roses. I tucked it into the paper around the flowers."

I shake my head. "I never saw a note."

My mind goes back to that summer day. I kept going back and forth to the car, packing everything for the trip down to North Carolina, Mom constantly calling out not to forget this or that. She went to the store for some last minute items, and then there was Eli, tall and lean, shoving a dozen red roses in my hand and saying he'd miss me.

I scrunch my brows, trying to remember what happened to the flowers after that. "I brought the flowers with me to the car because I thought they'd be nice in my new dorm, but Mom said they wouldn't survive the heat of the long trip. She took them inside for me to put them in a vase of water, and then we left." I lift my palms. "Maybe the note fell out somewhere along the way, or she accidentally threw it out with the paper in her rush to get on the road. She never mentioned seeing a note."

He leans back on the sofa, looks heavenward, and groans.

"What? What did it say?"

He closes his eyes. "I'm such an idiot. All that lost time when you came back to town."

I smack his shoulder. "You *were* avoiding me! I knew it!" My jaw gapes as I realize the implications. "It must've been something really embarrassing in that note. Did teenaged Eli write me a mushy love poem?"

He tackles me, and I shriek in surprise, laughing. He nuzzles into my neck, his stubbled jaw rubbing against me as his body covers mine. The friction is delicious, the sudden heat, his weight. I wrap my arms around his neck, all teasing gone.

He lifts his head, his voice gruff. "You were my dream girl. You've always been my dream girl."

My breath catches. "Eli, that's so—"

"Don't say nice."

I shake my head, my eyes wide with wonder. "It's the most amazing thing anyone has ever said to me."

His lips meet mine in a scorching kiss that steals my breath. Because it's not just a kiss, every movement, every urgent press of his lips and tongue feels like more. Like pent-up feelings expressed fully for the first time—passion, need, tenderness…love?

I tear my mouth away. "Eli, what did the note say?"

"Not now," he says hoarsely.

His warm hand cradles my jaw as he deepens the kiss. I grip his shirt, keeping him close, needing his kiss more than answers.

A long moment later, he gets off me and pulls me up with him. We stand there, staring into each other's eyes. My breath comes harder, every part of my body crying out for more. He's sexy and safe at the same time. Every guy I've ever been with is a risk because I don't know them that well. Will they be too aggressive, be a jerk, or otherwise suck? Eli does not suck. He's amazing.

I'm not sure who moves first, but we slam together. The kiss is scorching, his fingers tangled in my hair, his other hand cupping my ass, holding me close and setting off an urgent need in me that can't be denied. I'm on fire, fever hot. My hands go to the bottom of his shirt, yanking it up. He rips off his shirt and then kisses me long and deep, like he has all the time in the world. I'm making up for lost time, all the attraction I tried to deny, the feelings—it's all bubbling over.

I push at his chest, and he backs off instantly. I pull my shirt over my head.

He sucks in air. "Beautiful. The things I want to do to you."

"I want everything. Right now."

His arms wrap around me as he says low by my ear, "We have all night."

He bends his head, kissing the soft spot behind my ear and then lower, slowly moving along my neck. I slide my hands over his broad back, down his sides, enjoying the play of hard muscular ridges. My fingers still as his teeth scrape against me. He continues kissing along the column of my neck until he gets to a sensitive spot, and my knees buckle. I feel his lips curve against my neck, his hand sliding to the waistband of my pants, slipping underneath.

He undresses me in between kisses, and I return the favor as we make our way to his bedroom. He turns on the light, dimming it, and then guides me to his bed. He peels the covers back and gives me a small push. I land sitting on the mattress and look up at him.

His eyes gleam, his expression intent like a hunter who's finally caught up with his meal. My breath hitches. I have never seen a man look at me like that. Like he's ravenous for me.

He drops to his knees, pushes my legs apart, and looks his fill. I'm tempted to shift away, unprepared for such open intimacy. He traces me with his fingers, and it feels so good I don't mind so much that he's seeing me this way. And then he kisses me intimately, the reward so pleasurable that I drop back weakly onto the mattress, surrendering immediately. He hums his pleasure against me before taking me on a slow slide to languid pleasure. My hips rock of their own accord to the rhythm he's set as a fiery pleasure builds and builds.

He's good at this.

Great.

Oh God.

I break with a harsh cry, white-hot pleasure flooding me. I reach for him frantically. "I need you inside me."

He doesn't hesitate, grabbing a condom from his nightstand, and rolling it on.

I smile. "You came prepared."

"I didn't expect this, Jenna. I meant it when I said sex was off the table, but I had to consider the possibility."

"Don't apologize. I'm thrilled. And don't you dare stop now."

He enters me in a hard thrust that steals my breath. And then there's no more talk. I lift my hips, meeting him eagerly as he pounds into me. It's exactly what I need. Unbelievably, I can feel it building again. That never happens for me. One and done, and I'm grateful to get one at all. My world clouds, my vision blurring, sounds muted as sensations spiral tighter, hotter, the pressure building.

His fingers slip between my legs, stroking me expertly. *Too much.* I tremble under him.

He whispers in my ear, coaxing me in a husky voice, telling me he's going to get me there, that I need to relax and let him take control.

Sounds I've never made before come from my throat as he takes over, my mind shutting down, my body responding to his touch, his musky scent, the deep timbre of his voice, pushing me on and on.

The orgasm slams into me, my body shuddering with it, wave after wave of pleasure rushing through me. I go limp, dazed by it.

"Good, so good," he croons in my ear.

And then he keeps going, setting off fireworks of pleasure within me with every stroke. I'm panting, overwhelmed with sensation, rocked by him, until he finally lets go with a low groan. We stay like that for a long moment, pressed tight against each other, catching our breath.

The words are out before I can stop them. "I want more than two days."

He lifts his head, his hazel eyes sparkling. "Was it the second orgasm that tipped the scales?"

I cup his stubbled jaw, a surge of affection going through me. "It's you."

"Hmm, let me think about it." He rolls to his back, bringing me with him. I land on top of him with a laugh. His arms wrap around me, and he tucks my head against his chest. I let out a happy sigh.

He shifts and turns out the light, his arms securely wrapping around me again. I'm content, warm and drowsy. A lingering question hovers in my mind, and I summon my last bit of strength to lift my head. "Eli?"

"Yeah?" He sounds tired.

"Can you please tell me what the note said?"

He presses my head back to his chest. "Go to sleep, Jenna."

That's the last thing I remember.

10

Next thing I know, Lucy is licking my face. I give her a pet, get out of Eli's bed, and wander into the living room of the suite.

He's standing in the galley kitchen, his hair damp from the shower, wearing a black flannel shirt, jeans, and hiking boots. "Morning, beautiful."

My lips curve into a smile, my heart kicking hard. "Morning."

He claps his hands together. "Chop-chop. We've got apples to pick, leaves to peep at, and ice cream to eat."

I rush to his side, overcome with affection, and throw my arms around him in a hug. "That all sounds wonderful." *Just like you.*

He cups my jaw, smiling down at me. "Looks like kidnapping agrees with you."

I kiss him and take a step back, overwhelmed by all I'm feeling. Is this love? It's scary but good scary, like the thrill of a roller-coaster ride. "I'll shower and get dressed." I head toward my room.

"I'll get breakfast."

He's such a great guy. Maybe I was wrong all these years to hold part of myself back with guys. Or maybe only Eli would have this effect on me.

I turn back. "You're a real gem, you know that?"

His eyes are intent on mine. "Remember that when we go back to the real world."

My happiness dims at the thought. I'm not ready to think about reality. I hurry back to my room.

~

It's late, and I'm tired after a busy day spent hiking and apple picking. Maybe it's all that fresh air and sunshine catching up with me. Or maybe it's the double scoop of mint chocolate-chip ice cream I just ate, but I can't keep my eyes open. I doze off on the drive home as soon as the sun sets.

We stop for burgers for dinner, feeding some burger to Lucy, and continue home. This time I'm wide awake. I had a really good time with him, but I'm worried. I don't know how to navigate relationship territory. What's too much? Where are the boundaries?

He pulls into the driveway of my place and turns off the car. "I'll get your suitcase for you."

"Wait."

He looks at me, a question in his eyes.

"I had a great time. Thank you."

"Me too. I'm glad it worked out. Could've backfired with the kidnapping thing. On the other hand, Audrey agreed it was the only way to get you alone long enough to make a real connection."

My heart's in my throat. "Well, Audrey would know."

"Don't be mad at her. She knows you well and told me she wants you to be happy. Obviously she thought the two of us together was a good thing, or she wouldn't have helped out."

My eyes sting with unshed tears. I hardly ever cry. It's just that I feel connected to him, and I never thought I'd have that with anyone. "I have…feelings for you."

"Jenna." He rests his forehead against mine. "I know you do, but thank you for saying that."

I laugh a little. "It's like you know me or something." He's very observant. I guess that goes with the cop territory.

"Yeah, and vice versa, I hope."

I kiss him. "Do you want to spend the night, or is that too—"

"I'd love to. I'll get Lucy." He gets out of the car, lets Lucy out of the back seat, grabs my suitcase, and follows me upstairs.

Lucy sniffs around my living room before settling on the area rug next to my sofa.

I turn to him. "So, here we are." Somehow it feels different between us, and I'm not sure how to proceed.

He takes my hand and leads me to the bedroom, shutting the door behind us. "No doggy witnesses."

I smile. "Just us."

We reach for each other at the same time, and this time there's no hesitation. Just hungry kisses, voracious heat that flashes into an inferno. We tumble into bed for a heart-pounding ride.

And when we finish, he tucks me firmly against his side, his chest rising and falling as he catches his breath.

My mind works overtime on what happens next. Are Eli and I really a steady sure thing? Should I confess all to Sydney? Part of me feels like this new thing between us is too fragile to bring out in the open.

I stare at his profile, the angle of his masculine jaw, the way his lashes fan out on his cheeks when his eyes are closed. "So…I guess this means we're kinda dating?"

He kisses my hair. "I'll pick you up on Saturday for dinner and dancing over at Happy Endings."

It sounds so simple, so fun. And it's in Clover Park, which makes it easier to keep quiet about us. No judging eyes from Summerdale over there.

He opens his eyes and turns to me. "Okay?"

"Yes, okay. It's a date."

There must be a hint of anxiety in my voice because he rolls on top of me and nuzzles by my ear. "Don't worry, I'll be gentle."

I grab his shoulders. "We can only do this if it's in complete secrecy."

He lifts his head. "I don't think that's a good idea."

"We have to."

He hesitates, studying me. "Not for long."

I look away.

He holds my chin and forces my gaze back to his. "Secrets always come out. There's no reason for us to sneak around."

I push at his chest, but he doesn't budge. "Yes, there is."

He grabs one of my pushing hands and kisses the palm. "That's not going to work for long. You understand that, right?"

Who knows how long this thing will last between us? If it's short, there's no reason to cause a rift with Sydney. I'm taking a huge leap of faith even agreeing to a date.

He nips my lower lip. "Do you really need me to say the obvious? You are by far the hottest, sexiest woman I've met in my life, and I'm not done with you yet."

He lowers himself down my body, kissing, tasting, caressing. My resistance melts in a haze of ecstatic pleasure.

~

The rest of the week flies by between work and my responsibilities on the Fall Harvest committee. We meet on Tuesday nights, and I missed this week's meeting because I was driving home with Eli. Then there was a flurry of emails and phone calls catching me up. The committee is local shopkeepers; the mayor, who I grew up with; Levi; and a few interested citizens, General Joan being one of them. She recruited the high school jazz band to play for the dance-athon, which should be interesting. Will we be swing dancing?

Welp, I'll be dancing tonight. Right on cue, my stomach flutters, thinking of seeing Eli again. I swipe red lipstick across my lips. I'm still in a bit of shock over how quickly things progressed from kidnapping to connecting the way we did. I've never felt this way about any guy. And I'm excited to dance too. Audrey doesn't like to go to clubs, and Sydney's always working weekends at her restaurant.

I spritz on some perfume I love. It's floral with a hint of vanilla. Men love it and so do I. I'm wearing a black turtleneck and velvet green miniskirt with ankle boots.

Eli rings the bell a few minutes early. I put a hand over my heart, surprised at the acceleration. It's not like it's a first date. I should be a little calmer about seeing him by now.

I grab my black clutch and open the door. "Hello."

He takes me in from my hair to my red lips to a slow perusal of my outfit. "Very nice," he murmurs, and I feel the deep timbre of his voice down to my toes. His gaze makes a slow perusal back up my body, finally meeting my eyes again. "Beautiful."

"Thank you."

He leans in to kiss my cheek. He smells amazing, fresh and clean, his dark hair still damp from the shower. And he's wearing a leather jacket over a black T-shirt and jeans, bringing the edgy good guy I find myself craving into sharp focus.

"Ready?" he asks.

I nod and lead the way out.

When we get to his car, I check out the front. It was repaired this week. Thankfully the insurance company covered everything but the deductible. "They did good work on your car. It looks brand new."

He grimaces. "Not quite but close. Sloane says you're bringing your car in next week."

"Yeah, I figured I should for safety reasons." I plan to put it on my credit card and pay the minimum each month. One day I'll pay everything off. It takes time for a new business like mine to prosper.

He opens the passenger side door of his Mustang for me. Nerves skitter through me because it feels like we're an actual couple now.

I slide into the black leather seat, and he shuts the door behind me. Maybe I'll relax once we get to Clover Park. As soon as he gets in the car, I tell him, "I used to go to Happy Endings as a kid when it was Garner's."

"Did you like it?"

"Yeah." His car still has that new-car smell. "I'm really sorry I dinged your new car."

"Me too. But Trixie and I have recovered."

"That's the first time I've heard you call your car by name. Now it feels even more personal that I damaged her. Do you always name your cars?"

"Course. Doesn't everyone?" He turns it on, and the engine roars to life. "I was late on naming this one, and look what happened."

"I've never named my car. Not once."

He navigates the side streets, heading toward Route 15, which leads to Clover Park. "Well, you should. Your car might treat you better instead of getting into fender benders."

"That was user error."

"No question."

He pulls smoothly out onto Route 15 and hits the accelerator. I have to admit his car is a nice ride.

"So what's your deal, Jenna? Ever have a serious relationship, any baggage I should know about? Exes who might pop out of the woodwork?"

"Wow. Just jumping into the deep end here, are we? If we're asking questions, then I'd really like to know what was in that note that made you avoid me for a year."

"Fair enough," he says gamely. "I don't need to know about your past relationships."

I laugh. "How bad could it be? Roses are red, violets are blue, insert teenaged rhyme here?"

He clears his throat. "I don't remember exactly. It was so long ago."

I study him. He's got that neutral expression he's so good at. I'm suspicious, but I let it slide. "Since you're not sharing about that, tell me about *your* relationship history."

"This is feeling very one-sided in the sharing department. I just need to know if I'm going to have to use my ninja skills on one of your exes at some point."

I smile. "You don't have to worry about that. I never let it get that far, my choice."

"What do you mean by that far?"

"I mean, you know, relationship territory. Nothing more than a month since college and, according to my alumni magazine, he's married."

His brows lift. "Huh, okay. Well, guess it's my turn. You already know about Beatrice. Most people I've dated, it doesn't last long, just not enough in common or whatever, but I did date Rebecca for five months. I'm afraid I broke her heart when I broke up with her."

"Why did you?"

"I just wasn't happy. Like I didn't get excited about seeing her. She complained a lot too."

"So you dropped her whiny ass. Can't blame you."

"She's married now. So you and me, we're both kind of a clean slate. No baggage, no exes bound to pop up."

"I guess."

"Favorite sex position?"

I do a double take.

He grins.

I squeeze his thigh. "You'll have to find that out the hard way."

He grabs my hand and kisses my knuckles. "That's the way I like it best too."

~

We're seated at a booth by the front window of Happy Endings with a view of Main Street, which is a tree-lined street with lots of cute shops. Happy Endings is a bar and restaurant with an addition in back for dancing and a couple of pool tables too. After a delicious dinner of fried chicken and mashed potatoes, Eli asks me if I'd like to go for a walk after eating.

I push back my plate. "Absolutely. I need to work off some of this fried chicken."

"Great, because they don't start the jukebox in the back room until nine."

"A jukebox?"

"Yeah, it's cool. A vintage machine that plays vinyl."

I slide out of the booth. "Not much of a club feel here, I guess."

He joins me. "More like you can actually talk to each other, and there's no fog machine smoking up the place."

"Should be interesting."

He places his palm on the small of my back, guiding me toward the door. My skin heats at the spot, and I suddenly want those big hands on more of me. "I come here regularly. It's a great place to meet people because you can actually see and hear each other."

"Will we run into one of your exes?" I ask over my shoulder.

He opens the front door for me. "I wouldn't notice when I'm with you."

I nearly stumble on my way out, but he catches my arm, steadying me. *The things he says.*

We start walking down the street. I'm barely aware of my surroundings, so caught up in the dreamy state of wonder that Eli weaves around me.

A happy-looking couple walks toward us, eating ice-cream cones. There's something familiar about them.

I squint and then freeze, grabbing Eli's arm to halt him.

"What's wrong?"

I grip him tighter, my heartbeat roaring in my ears. "My parents. Here." They must've just walked out of Shane's Scoops. My God, they look like they're on a date. After the war that was their divorce with all the devastation that wrought, they're on a frigging date?

My vision tunnels to their smiling faces, the world falling away. Do I pretend I didn't see them or say hello?

"Jenna!" Mom calls. "What a surprise. I didn't know you still spent time here. Remember we used to have brunch at Garner's when you girls were little? Well, Happy Endings now, but they still offer brunch."

Brunch? She's talking about brunch? This is not happening.

"Eli?" Mom asks when she reaches us. She hasn't seen him in a while since she moved out of town when I left for college.

She sold our house and moved into an apartment. Not in Clover Park either. This is too freaky to run into them here.

Eli offers his hand. "Yes, ma'am, good to see you again." He shakes Dad's hand too.

My mouth is dry. "What's going on?"

My parents look at each other with a doe-eyed look before turning back to me.

"We reconnected," Mom says with a smile.

"Evie moved to California for a job, and I was missing her," Dad says. "I got in touch with your mom to talk about it. We're both empty nesters now. Anyway—" he takes her hand "—we had a good talk."

"And we decided to forgive and forget," Mom says.

"Forgive and forget," I echo incredulously. *After the hell you put me and Evie through?*

Mom glances at Eli before turning back to me. "We should talk. I'll call you."

I hold up a palm. "I have to go." I tug Eli's hand, turning us back the way we came, and walk away at a brisk pace. "Forget dancing," I tell him. "I'm heading for the bar."

"That was weird," he says.

"Ya think? My parents are dating. Not what you want to see after a hellish divorce."

As soon as we get inside Happy Endings, I make a beeline for the bar. The bartender, a laidback-looking guy in his thirties with tousled brown hair and a scruffy jaw, wearing a flannel shirt with jeans, gives me a smile. "What can I get you?"

I plop down on a barstool. "Two tequilas and keep 'em coming."

Eli joins me. "Are you okay?"

"I can't believe this. After they destroyed my childhood, tore apart my family, gave away my dog…" My voice chokes. No wonder I'm so screwed up when it comes to relationships.

Eli tucks an arm around my shoulders and pulls me close. I'm too mad to cry, but I let him hold me for a moment before pulling away.

My drinks arrive, and I down the first shot and reach for the second. Eli grabs it out of my hand.

"This one has my name on it," he says, tossing it back.

"Hey, Josh, can we get two more beers?" a handsome dark-haired guy with olive skin and a charming smile asks from the other end of the bar. He's sitting with a guy with sandy brown hair and a T-shirt that says Elegant Land Designs.

"Coming up, Rico." Josh gets to work on their beers, but I really think my tequila takes precedence.

"When you're done with their order, can we get a couple more shots, please?" I ask Josh.

"Just water for me," Eli tells him. He turns to me. "I'm driving."

Josh inclines his head. "Sure thing."

He hands over their beer and returns to us, taking our empty shot glasses and tucking them under the bar.

"Daddy!" a little girl squeals, running toward the bar. She looks about five with honey brown hair that falls over her shoulders, wearing pink and white polka-dotted pajamas with sneakers.

Josh's face lights up. "Mackenzie, my girl." He comes around the bar to lift her in the air, saying over her shoulder, "Cooper the Super! Hailey, my warrior princess. What're you all doing here at bedtime?"

"They wanted Daddy before story time," the warrior princess mom says. She's a stunning blonde woman, holding a boy on her hip with the same honey brown hair as his sister. He's in Superman pajamas complete with a cape. Probably around three years old. The mom doesn't dress like a typical suburban mom. She looks like she just stepped off the runway in a fitted navy sheath dress with knee-high black leather boots.

"Me, me," Cooper says.

Josh puts Mackenzie down and scoops up Cooper, flying him under one arm in a fast circle. The boy beams as he flies around. Josh sets him down and smiles at his wife, murmuring something in a low tone.

Hailey smiles, stepping close to speak to him softly.

My throat tightens watching this happy family. Now Josh has a kid hanging off each arm as he listens to his wife. *Was my family ever that happy?*

More people approach the bar.

Josh glances back toward the bar. "Hailey, I got to…"

Hailey nods once. "I'll let you go back to work. Tell Daddy goodnight."

"Goodnight, Daddy!" Cooper shouts.

"Inside voice, Coop," Hailey says.

"Goodnight, Daddy," Cooper whispers and then shouts, "Bye!" He tears through the back of the restaurant, heading through the double doors that lead to the kitchen. His mom runs after him.

Eli whispers in my ear, "That boy reminds me of me."

I grin. "I was thinking the same thing."

Mackenzie rolls her eyes, parking a hand on her hip. "He always runs off, Daddy. We need to put a leash on him like Rose and Max."

"Your brother is not a dog," Josh says with a chuckle, ruffling her hair. "Wait for Mommy to come back with him."

A moment later, Hailey walks in, hair disheveled, her dress slightly askew, Cooper securely gripped on her hip. "He was climbing the kitchen counter because he wanted to help make salad."

"Mommy likes salad," Cooper says as though it's obvious why he had to climb the counter.

Josh shakes his head. "Coop, you stay out of the restaurant kitchen unless Mommy or Daddy is with you."

Cooper looks solemn. "Okay."

"Bye, Daddy," Mackenzie says.

"Bye, munchkin," Josh says.

Mackenzie skips over to her mom and takes her hand.

My chest aches. How awesome would it be to have a warm loving husband and happy kids with smiles all around? I don't have a clue how this couple made that happen, but part of me is jealous that they have the kind of family I always wished I had as a kid. Of course, that dream died long ago when I got a grip on reality. It's rare what they have.

Josh goes behind the bar and gets busy serving up drinks. Fortunately, he remembers we were next and promptly gives us our drinks before helping the new customers.

Eli and I clink glasses. I toss back my shot, and he sips his water, watching me over the rim of his glass.

"Happy family," I whisper to him.

He leans close. "Looks that way."

"Your family was happy before your mom died. I remember that."

He gets serious, and I instantly regret my words. I put a hand on his chest. "I'm so sorry. I shouldn't have said that." I'm sure he doesn't like to be reminded of his mom's death. Geez, what is wrong with me?

"It's okay," he says, placing his hand over mine, keeping it against his chest. "My parents were close. We knew they loved us. I hope to have the same one day."

I pull my hand away, my mind buzzing with a hornet's nest of nasty warning signals. I'm in over my head with Eli. My parents' drama is too fresh in my mind. I call over to Josh, "One more tequila, please."

Huge mistake.

Within minutes of finishing my drink, my buzz takes a dive into despair, devastated all over again by my screwed-up family. I tell Eli to bring me home.

Then I confess all the garbage my parents put me and my sister through on the ride home. I finish just as we pull into my driveway.

He's quiet.

He knows *everything*. How badly my parents messed me up, how they took away my sister, how I lost my beloved dog.

I can't bear it. "I'm not feeling well. You should go."

The date is officially ruined. So is whatever fledgling relationship we had. It's too late. I can't take back my ugly confession.

I get out of the car and make my way blindly to the stairs leading to my apartment, tears blurring my vision. Eli's arm suddenly wraps around my side, walking with me.

I push his arm away, and he puts it back, guiding me upstairs. I can't find the strength to resist him.

11

I wake fully dressed in my bed with the hangover from hell. Slowly, I become aware of heat, shift my arm, and make contact with a large male body by my side. Eli. I peek under the covers. He's only wearing blue boxer briefs.

Last night comes flooding back to me, my parents dating, drinking too much, telling Eli everything, all the gory details I've never told any guy. I cover my face with my hands, beyond embarrassed. I can't believe he spent the night after all that. He probably wanted to wait for me to sleep off the alcohol before gently breaking the news that he no longer feels *that way* about me. I never should've let it get this far anyway. I don't know what I was thinking. I wasn't thinking. That's the problem.

I drop my hands, keeping my eyes closed. My parents were so casual about getting back together too. It just proves that people can't be trusted. They've never acknowledged the damage they did. I don't think I can salvage this thing with Eli with all the crap in my head and the way he must see me now. It's laughable that he ever saw me as his dream girl. This sucks so bad. I like him a lot and was just starting to feel hopeful.

I rub my temples. My head is killing me.

I slowly maneuver to a sitting position, pushing the

tangled hair out of my face. Eli rolls to his back, his bare chest above the sheet, exposing the defined muscular lines of his shoulders and pecs. I'll miss that. I'll miss him. Why did I have to ruin it by sharing all the ugly parts of my life?

I swing my legs over to the side of the mattress and slowly get out of bed. My tongue feels fuzzy. I shuffle to the bathroom and get ready in slow motion so I don't jar my head, including a long swishing session with mouthwash before making my way to the kitchen for water and some medicine for this headache. *Why do I store medicine in the kitchen cabinet instead of the bathroom?* A question for non-hungover Jenna to handle. Probably lack of space.

"Hey, how're you feeling?" Eli asks.

I halt in my tracks. He's standing in my kitchen, fully dressed in the black T-shirt and jeans from last night, the coffee maker percolating behind him. *How long was I in the bathroom?*

"Coffee," I whisper. "Bless you."

He studies me, his expression serious. "Guess you're hungover pretty bad."

I nod and instantly regret it. I take a couple of pills and lean against the counter, guzzling water. And then I help myself to coffee, adding a cube from the sugar jar I keep on the counter. This is going to be hard, but I have to face last night in the harsh light of day.

I wrap my hands around the thick white mug and take a fortifying sip. "Eli, I'm beyond embarrassed that you saw me like that. And I so regret unloading all that garbage on you."

His voice is soft, his hazel eyes full of concern. "You're a sad drunk. It must've been a shock to see your parents together after their bitter divorce. I've heard of people who divorce and marry the same person multiple times."

I look up at him, surprised to hear that. "They're definitely not getting married again."

"I guess they're the reason you don't want to get married. You did say you haven't had any long-term relationships, so I know it's not because of an ex that you feel that way."

My lower lip quivers. He's so intuitive and smart, putting

all the pieces together. The obvious conclusion is the elephant in the room—he wants marriage one day, just like his happy parents and his older sister and brother, and he deserves to be with someone who wants the same thing. That was Sydney's point all along about why we didn't suit each other. It was so foolish of me to pretend otherwise because now ending it hurts way too much.

He sets his mug on the counter. "Jenna," he says gently.

I can't bear to hear him break the news in soft tones, so I beat him to it. "This was a mistake. I don't think we should see each other anymore. We want different things, and that's not fair to you."

"What different things?"

"You deserve someone who can give you the whole pretty picture. You know, the house with a wife and kids." My voice cracks. "Someone like Brooke."

"Would you stop bringing up Brooke?" he snaps. "Just because Sydney wants to set me up with her doesn't mean I want her. I met her *once* at Sydney's wedding."

I wince at his volume. "Sorry, but you know what I mean. Someone like her, someone not so damaged." I swallow hard. "It's over."

"Why? Give me one good reason."

He sounds angry. *Doesn't he see I'm only trying to save him from future hurt?*

"Because I'm not what you need," I say quietly.

His eyes flash. "Why do you get to say what I need? How do you even know?"

I set my mug down. "Don't you see this is the only way? I don't want to hurt you."

He sets his mug down. "Too late." He walks out of the kitchen, stops, and turns around. "You know, I don't judge you for having messed-up parents, but I think you're a coward for using them as an excuse not to be with me."

I can barely speak over the lump of emotion lodged in my throat. "How dare you. I told you *everything,* and you use it against me."

He shakes his head. "No, it's exactly the reverse. You're

using this shit against *me*. That's why I think you're a coward."

"I'm not a coward!"

"Bye, Jenna." His brows furrow for a moment before he turns on his heel and walks out.

A hornet's nest of thoughts immediately buzzes in my brain—my parents getting together, the loss of my sister in my life, Eli judging me so harshly after I spilled my guts. I put both hands to my head, willing it to quiet down in there. I need a hot shower. I'll deal with all this later.

Only when I'm under the steamy spray, it's the hurt in Eli's eyes I can't get out of my mind.

Eli

The next morning I'm still pissed off. Jenna dumped me for no good reason after asking me to spend the night! She was drunk when she asked, but still. Things were great between us until she saw her parents, and guess what? They have nothing to do with us. The worst part is—the part that makes me feel like I'm walking around with my heart flapping in the wind—this whole thing between us has been lopsided from the beginning. Not only because I've had a fantasy about being with Jenna since I was a teen, because I admitted it. I never should've done that. My pride is wounded just as much as my heart.

My younger brother, Caleb, wanders into the kitchen, shirtless and barefoot in jeans to make his usual green smoothie. We share the two-story colonial home we grew up in. Dad left the house to all of us, but Drew and Adam already owned their own homes, and Sydney wanted to live in the apartment over The Horseman Inn for convenience. Now she lives with her husband, Wyatt, across town. Caleb's got an apartment in the city too, so he comes and goes according to whenever he has a modeling gig there. He also works part time at our brother Drew's dojo.

"Morning," he says, chipper as usual. He's one of those

people born with a permanently sunny disposition. Nothing gets him down. Is that why women are drawn to him in droves? It's been that way forever. Even in elementary school, he had a harem of girls trailing him around. Sure, he's good looking with his light brown hair in a buzz cut and his clean-shaven face with a sunny smile, but no more than any of us Robinsons. Pretty sure it's something else that attracts women to him like a magnet. I don't need a harem. I just want one woman who's as into me as I'm into her. Is that so much to ask?

"Morning," I grumble. My pit bull Lucy rests her head on my leg and looks up at me with concern in her brown eyes. She's a beauty with a short light brown coat with white fur on her chest, front paws, and the top of her muzzle. I rub her side, and she leans against me heavily, comforting me.

"What's up?" Caleb asks. "You sound grumpier than usual for morning."

"Nothing." Jenna and I hadn't gone public yet, so I can't go around sharing the news that we had a thing that's now over. I was so sure it was the start of something real. She was upset when she ended it, like she was in pain. And I called her a coward.

I run a hand through my hair. Maybe I need to be more patient. I never had to deal with the family drama she did.

Caleb takes kale, carrots, and leeks from the refrigerator. "Want some smoothie?"

I fight my gag reflex at the thought. "No, thanks, I'm good with coffee."

He throws it together with some ice, the blender making a racket, while I stew. He pours a tall glass of dark green smoothie and takes a long drink, eyeing me over the glass.

I'm done with my coffee and should get ready for work, but I linger. It's not that I need advice from my younger brother. It's just that this Jenna thing is a puzzle I need to solve.

"I'm not asking for advice," I start, considering my words carefully.

Caleb gestures me on, wiggling his fingers and leaning back against the counter. "Hit me."

"There's this woman. We had a good time together, went out a few times, and then she cut ties." I look out the window over the sink at the bright autumn leaves in the backyard, remembering our trip together. "Everything had been great before that."

"She just broke up with you for no reason? Maybe there was another guy."

"No, nothing like that. She had a family issue."

She made assumptions about my expectations, our future, the hopelessness of it all. And then my back got up because I had admitted how much I was into her. *My dream girl.* I grimace.

"And?" he prompts.

I stare at the table, trying to get some perspective on this. "I think I was just caught in the fray." I meet his hazel eyes, so like my own. I haven't talked to Jenna since then. Maybe she's as miserable as I am. "You think she overreacted and regrets ending it with me?" My entire face burns. God, I sound pathetic. This is the problem with being hung up on someone for so long. I'm forever in the pursuer position. I want her to pursue me for once to prove it's not all me here mired in deep-feelings territory.

He shakes his head. "Doubtful, but who knows? I have the opposite problem. Women always want to stick with me. It's like the less I want to get involved, the more they want me." He doesn't sound torn up about it.

"And you never felt the same way back?"

"Nope. I'm happy with my life just like it is." He tosses back more dark green smoothie. Maybe it's the phytochemicals drawing women to him. I can't go there, even for Jenna. Gross.

Jenna did say she's never had a serious relationship—her choice. Still, I can't help but want to be the one who makes her see things differently. It could be worth seeing each other again. Right?

I stare at the table. Or maybe I'm just too hung up on her to face the harsh truth—she's not as into me as I'm into her.

"Is it Jenna?" he asks.

My head jerks up. "How did you know?"

He grins. "We used to share a room. I saw you spraying on cologne every time she came over. You've had a thing for her forever. Plus your whole face lit up when you told me about your parking lot accident with her, almost like you were happy it happened. Sicko."

A happy accident.

"I wasn't." I focus on my coffee, not really seeing it. "Of course I wasn't."

"Just do what I do. Move on. Don't pay her any attention at all. If she's interested, she'll be right there in front of you when you least expect it."

"So let her come to me."

He lifts his glass in a toast to that. "Exactly. Nothing worse than a chase with someone who doesn't want to be caught."

He's a little too close to my worst-case humiliating scenario. "And you know this how?" I snap.

He grins. "I'm the one who's always chased."

~

Jenna

I'm at my table for the Fall Harvest Festival a full week after ending things with Eli, and I'm still miserable. I hurt him, and that was the last thing I wanted to do. *I miss him.*

I miss his warm smile, his confident take-charge attitude, the way he made me feel, like I was something special. I've barely slept at all. I spend too much time in my head, replaying everything with Eli. Well, I can't take it back now. And nothing's changed, really. I'm trying to be practical for both our sakes. That's not a cowardly act. It's selfless. If I was being selfish, I would've hung onto him as long as possible because he made me feel so good, even knowing it would end in catastrophe.

It's for the best.

I swallow hard and try to focus on my surroundings. The air is filled with the delicious scent of my own fresh-baked double fudge cookies, along with grilled burgers, hot dogs, and chicken from the nearby tent run by The Horseman Inn. It's the last Saturday of September, and there's a good crowd on this gorgeous fall day. The air is crisp, the sky a perfect blue with white fluffy clouds, and fall leaves are both overhead and on the ground.

Kids are crunching through the leaves with their faces painted, stopping by the various tents and tables from local shopkeepers, the library, and a few craftsmen. The lawn next to the Presbyterian church is set up with more kiddy fun—games, a bouncy house, and an inflatable slide. There's a playground too for little kids, part of the church's preschool. Their laughter lifts my spirits.

Summerdale has two churches—Presbyterian and Episcopalian—at opposite ends of Peaceable Lane with rival preschools. People say the Presbyterian preschool is strict, and the Episcopalian preschool is run by a bunch of wannabe hippies. You enroll your kid based on personality. Sydney's family went to the Presbyterian preschool because her mom went to church there. Sydney always said there would've been a lot less calls home to her mom about Eli and Caleb if she'd broken rank and enrolled them in the hippie version of preschool. Ha. Troublemaker Eli.

Good guy Eli.

Dammit. I miss him way too much.

Customers await! I serve up some brownies and cookies to a couple of young families at my table. A bunch of older kids arrive with cash wadded in their hands, ready to devour my treats. Everyone's in good spirits. I work hard to be cheerful, pushing the pain down. It probably doesn't help that my parents both called me several times this week. I've ignored every call, not ready to deal with the fact of their dating. I'm curious what my sister's take is on it. She was just as affected by the custody tug-of-war and the fallout. She was forced to visit with Mom and remained cool to her. My family is so messed up.

A familiar deep voice sounds from nearby. "Girls, out of the tree. We don't want anyone getting hurt."

My heart lurches. Eli stands a short distance away in his crisp blue uniform, watching as two girls obediently climb down from a young oak tree. I open my mouth to call out to him, but he turns away, continuing his walk through the festival, keeping an eye on things.

I let out a breath, my body suddenly so heavy I sink down onto a metal folding chair.

A trio of girls run up to the table, clutching cash. "Can we have some cookies?" they chorus.

I nod at them, and they check out all the offerings, chattering to each other about what to get. They're probably nine years old, wearing sparkly barrettes in their hair.

I stand and get back to helping my customers. Keeping busy is the best distraction.

I spend hours serving up cookies, cupcakes, and brownies as I watch the goings-on at the festival. I spot Eli a few times, always with his back to me. Audrey's across the street at the library, where she's set out several long tables for a book sale, mostly from donations and worn library books. Doing a brisk business over there. A bunch of kids are jumping in a bouncy house and then running to an inflatable slide. The games are popular with families with young kids. There's fishing for a magnetic fish in a kiddy pool, swirling sand art, and a lollipop game where they get to choose a lollipop from a large wooden board to win a prize based on a number taped to the stick. It seems everyone leaves that game with a lollipop.

I remember playing these same games as a kid, holding hands with my little sister, and then later running around with Sydney, Audrey, and Harper. Summerdale is a great place to grow up, a great place to raise kids. Low crime, high quality of life. Bike paths wind through the community, around the lake, and on each street. As long as you don't venture onto busy Route 15, a kid can pretty much go anywhere.

I wave at Sydney across the way, helping to serve up food for The Horseman. She's too busy to notice me.

A group of six teenaged boys crowds the front of my table, laughing and jabbing each other in the ribs. I recognize Chris. He's a busboy at The Horseman. Good kid.

I smile at them. "Hi, Chris and friends, what can I get you?"

A redheaded boy speaks up. "You're the big working man, Chris. This should be on you."

"I told you I'm saving for a car," Chris says. "One double fudge cookie, please, and a bottled water."

I serve them up, take his hard-earned cash, and then help his friends in a flurry of orders. They buy a lot of cookies. I'm going to have to go back to my shop to refill on the chocolate chip after this line dies down. I look up at my next customer and freeze.

The tall boys had blocked the view of my parents. They're holding hands, apparently waiting in line to see me.

I hold up a palm. "Whatever this is, no. I'm busy."

"We tried calling you, but you don't return our calls," Mom says.

I try for a deep breath but can't manage it, my heartbeat's roaring in my ears. "I'm not on board with this. I don't want to hear about you two being together, and I definitely don't want to see it."

"But, Jenna, we're getting remarried," Dad says.

A high-pitched ringing in my ears drowns out the rest. Mom's mouth is moving, but I can't hear a thing. The world swims in front of my eyes, and then everything goes black.

~

I slowly come to, lying down somewhere shady. I hear Audrey's gentle voice.

"Wake up, Jenna. Come on, sweetie."

I focus on her kind blue eyes. "What happened?"

"You had a shock," Mom says from my other side.

"You fainted," Audrey says.

Dad's standing by my feet, staring at me with a concerned expression. I'm on a stretcher in the shade by the ambulance.

Mike, one of our EMTs, approaches, and Mom joins Dad to give Mike room. I keep my focus on Mike as he asks me a series of medical questions. I can feel my parents staring at me.

I sit up. "I'm fine. Thanks for the concern. I just forgot to eat lunch." I turn to Audrey. "Who's watching my table?"

"I called Cecilia." That's my assistant, who was working at the shop. If she's at my tent now, then that means my shop is closed.

"I'm okay. I'll go back to the shop and reopen it."

"We'll go with you," Dad says. "Just to be sure you're okay."

It's because of you I'm not okay!

I get off the stretcher and grab Audrey's shoulder to steady myself. "No, Dad. This is not a good time."

"When is a good time?" Mom asks. "Just tell us and we'll be there."

How about never?

"I need to get to work."

Audrey puts a protective arm around my waist, bless her, even though she's eight inches shorter than me. It's more a show of solidarity than physical support as we walk down the lane to my shop.

"What the hell is going on with your parents?" she whispers. "Back together after Armageddon? They nearly destroyed each other and you."

"Right? The last thing I remember before I passed out is they said they're getting remarried."

"Get out!" She looks over her shoulder at them. "They're watching us walk away. Geez, I would've passed out too. You lost your sister and your dog, and you might as well have lost your dad for the few times you saw him because they couldn't get their shit together, and now this? It's wrong, wrong, wrong."

"I know." It's all I can manage with the tightness in my throat, but I feel vindicated. I'm not overreacting. Audrey knows. There's something seriously off here.

We get back to my shop, and I go behind the counter,

already starting to feel better. It's cool in the shop, I'm surrounded by my favorite scents and kitchen tools, and there's a counter barrier if I need it.

Audrey guides me to the stool behind the counter. "You should sit while you're here. I'm sure you're not going to have a ton of people passing through with the festival going on."

"I have to be open just in case." I take a seat. "Anyway, don't worry, I'm not going to pass out again. I'm fine now. It was just the shock, and I haven't been sleeping much, so I'm not my usual energetic self."

"Because of Eli?" she asks gently.

I nod. I told her what happened. She was the only one who knew I'd been seeing him at all.

She strokes my hair. "I don't think you should do the dance-athon later. When the festival winds down, you should have a nice relaxing dinner at home. I'll bring some wine, and we can chill."

"Aud, it's a fundraiser, and I know you signed up for it too. I'll just take a quick nap after I close, and I'll be good to go. You'll be with me there, so will Sydney and Kayla, and it's not like my parents are going to participate. They're too old."

Her brows knit together. "They're not that old. Forty-something, right?"

I stand, grab a rag, and clean the already clean counter. "Whatever. They only came here to tell me their big news. Now that they told me, there's nothing more to talk about."

"You have to face them sometime."

I scrub harder. "I don't want any part of this couple thing, and I'm certainly not going to their wedding. There's really no point in even talking about it. As far as I'm concerned, this whole thing never happened."

"Denial won't help," she says under her breath.

I toss the rag down. "We all do what we have to do." I flash my teeth in an approximation of a smile.

Audrey gestures for me to sit down again. I huff but I comply. She leans down and kisses my forehead. "I'm here for you no matter what."

I blink back tears and nod.

"Are you going to be okay here alone? I can call—"

Just then Sydney bursts in. "Your parents are certifiable! I want to dump ice water on their heads and kick their asses on their way out of town."

I smile for real this time. "Yeah, Aud, I'll be okay. Sydney's going to do the dirty work for me."

Audrey grins and heads out the door, giving Sydney's shoulder a squeeze on her way out. Audrey has to run the book sale, which is a fundraiser for the library.

Sydney joins me behind the counter, jamming her hands on her hips. "And to just show up here, springing it on you like that!"

"Actually, I ran into them in Clover Park last weekend, where it looked like they were on a date. They've been calling me ever since. I've been avoiding their calls, so I guess I should've expected they'd just show up."

"I'm furious on your behalf," Sydney says. "You owe them nothing. Don't even waste a single moment thinking about it."

I give her a watery smile. "I love you, lady."

"Love you too." She scowls. "Of all the nerve. What do they think, that you'll be happy for them?"

It's so good to know she has my back. Audrey too. "I have no idea what they're thinking."

She points at me. "You text me if they pop up on you again, and I'm there. We're a united front against any and all interlopers."

I laugh at her funny turn of phrase, and she throws an arm around me in a sideways hug.

"You're the best," I tell her.

"Don't you forget it. Sisters for life."

I blink back tears, thankful all over again for my best friends.

12

I'm glad I made the effort to go to the dance-athon, despite today's events, because now I'm having fun dancing with my friends. I changed into a swingy A-line yellow floral dress with black high heels. Thankfully, my parents aren't here. Eli is though, out of uniform, wearing a light blue button-down shirt, open at the collar, with jeans and loafers. We never did get to dance together. He caught my eye the moment I walked in, and jerked his chin at me. I debated walking over to say hi, but settled for a wave. He's over by the refreshment table now with his younger brother, Caleb.

The big red barn is decorated with twinkle lights along the ceiling, as well as fall harvest decorations. The entrance and three corners of the barn feature decorative displays of hay bales, pumpkins, and cornstalks. There's even a scarecrow wearing a red plaid shirt and denim overalls. The high school jazz band is parked in another corner.

Everyone humors General Joan, who's shouting into a megaphone as she patrols the dance floor in the center, organizing us into the twist, the swim, and the bunny hop. She doesn't know how to call out a square dance and was unsuccessful in getting our gym teacher, Mr. Perez, out of retirement to do the honors.

Finally, General Joan takes a break when the jazz band

packs up to go. They only had an hour's worth of songs to play for us. Their music teacher has a DJ setup in place and moves to his new station to keep the music going, playing a song I love with a fast-moving beat. I throw myself into it, and Eli and Caleb join us. Caleb moves closer to Audrey, who's got a sensual rhythm, and Eli dances near me. Sydney and Wyatt are off getting a drink with Kayla and Adam.

I shift closer, pitching my voice above the music, and attempt a friendly tone. "Off duty so soon?"

"Yup. I took day shift; the chief took night. Usually it's reversed, but he had his granddaughter's baptism earlier today and didn't want to miss it. Anyone gets out of hand here in the barn, he can take 'em. He's checking in on the latest with the General. She knows all, sees all."

Maybe we can be friends after all. He doesn't sound angry with me anymore.

I smile. "I can't imagine who would get out of hand on the General's watch."

We glance over at Mrs. Ellis sitting on a folding chair up on a raised dais, keeping a keen eye on everyone as she fills in Chief Daniels on the latest. She looks like a queen overseeing her subjects.

Eli takes my hand and spins me around, then draws me close, fast dancing with me in a quick box step before dipping me over one arm. I squeak in surprise, my arm flailing.

He draws me back up, his gaze smoldering into mine. My body craves contact. The rest of the world falls away. We're still moving but slower now, getting closer together.

"More space between you two!" General Joan barks into her megaphone, narrowing her eyes at us.

I jump, my gaze instantly searching for Sydney. She's too busy talking and laughing with Wyatt, Kayla, and Adam to pay any mind to the General. I shouldn't feel so guilty. It was just a friendly dance.

Eli moves behind me, still dancing, probably hiding from the General.

I turn to face him. "You're a good dancer."

"You're all arms and legs," he returns.

I gasp in mock outrage. "I wasn't expecting you to dip me."

Audrey appears by my side, grabs my arm, and whispers in my ear, "Your parents are here. They're talking to the DJ."

I mutter a curse. Now I have two choices—pretend like everything's fine or make a break for it. I don't want to talk about their ridiculous wedding. Two people could not be more ill-suited for remarrying.

I glance over at them. They're probably requesting a sappy love song. My gut churns, bile rising in my throat. Sydney's heading this way, which means I need to keep my distance from Eli. Shit. *What to do, what to do.*

Eli's brows furrow over concerned eyes. He speaks by my ear. "You look like you'd like to be kidnapped right about now."

"Yes!"

I take the lead, skirting the dance floor, Eli close behind. We make it all the way to the open barn doors before we're stopped by a stern Mrs. Ellis blocking our way, arms crossed. Even the General can't stand in my way this time.

"I hope you're not going to hide behind the barn," she says. "It's a bad example for two such prominent members of the community, especially a police officer." She narrows her eyes. "There are children here, you know."

I'm brought right back to my teen years, sneaking around with a boy. "Bye, Mrs. Ellis. Don't tell my parents what a bad girl I am. They're dancing over there, and I'm out of here."

Her jaw drops. "Your parents? Together?"

"Disgusting, isn't it?"

I don't wait for a reply, rushing past her and out of the barn, taking a deep breath of cool air.

"Jenna!"

I whirl to face Sydney, my heart beating double time.

"Where are you going?" she asks, looking from me to Eli and back again. "What's going on?"

My words tumble out in a rush. "My parents showed up. I'm just getting some air."

"With Eli?" she asks tightly. "How about—"

Eli cuts her off. "I'm taking her for a drive. Nothing better than a drive in a convertible to clear the head. Better go back in before the General thinks we're throwing a party out here. Can't be setting a bad example for the kids."

Sydney doesn't laugh; instead she turns to me. "I can take you for a drive."

"You don't have a convertible," I say. "I really need to go before my parents see me." I turn and walk briskly through the parking lot, Eli by my side. I don't dare look over my shoulder, but I can feel her eyes on me. It's just a ride. We're not even together anymore, but part of me feels like I've betrayed her by not admitting everything that went on before. There's no point now!

A few minutes later, we're on our way. Eli puts the convertible top down for our drive through a neighboring town over windy roads, past horse farms with rolling green hills, and the occasional home. I shake my hair out in the breeze. It's wonderful. Exactly what I needed. Slowly, the tension drains from me.

I turn to him. "I feel like I can breathe again."

His lips curve up in a small smile. "Good. Breathing's important. Music?"

"Yes!"

He turns on the radio, blasting a classic rock station. I tap my fingers in time to the music, taking in the beauty of the setting sun, streaks of orange and pink across the sky, when a song comes on that gets me singing, Cheap Trick's "I Want You To Want Me."

I turn in surprise because Eli's singing it too with real enthusiasm. The lyrics suddenly mean more. He wants me to want him, and I do. I really do.

He turns down the music after a while. "It's getting dark. Where to after this? You want me to drop you at home or…"

"Yeah, that sounds good." I know that's the right thing to do, even though I don't want our time together to end just yet.

He gets serious. "Sure, no problem."

He pulls into someone's driveway, backs into the street,

and turns the car back toward Summerdale. Fun time's over. I'm quiet the rest of the way home. My mind is whirling, agitated by my parents and everything they put me through only to get back together in the end. It brings back a cold fury I haven't felt in a very long time.

Eli pulls into my driveway, turns off the car, and turns to me. "You okay?"

"Yeah, I will be. Thanks for the fast escape. I guess I'll get my car from the barn tomorrow."

"I could give you a ride over there."

"No, I don't want to risk a run-in with my parents."

"Okay."

Our eyes lock for a moment, the longing in me making it difficult to look away. *Be strong*. I tear my gaze away. "Well, good night." I open the car door, but something prevents me from getting out. I turn back to him. "Would you like—"

"Yes."

I laugh a little. "You don't even know what I was going to say."

"I like whatever you're offering."

I smile. "Okay, then."

I get out of the car, and he joins me, following me upstairs to my apartment entrance. Once inside, I go straight to the kitchen. He follows me.

"Wine okay?"

His hazel eyes are intent on mine. "Sure."

I open a cabernet I keep in a cabinet with my liquor stash. He leans against the counter nearby, and I'm hyperaware of him as I get out two wineglasses and pour. *What am I doing?*

I rest both hands on the kitchen counter, drop my head, and sigh. "Tonight's been rough. I'm not sure I'm good company."

His arms wrap around me from behind, and it feels so good I let him. "I get it. You're dealing with a lot of family stuff."

I'm not ready to talk about it, so I just turn in his arms and lean against him. For once I'm not towering over a guy. I'm five nine and, even in heels like tonight, we still fit.

I lift my head, remembering the song we belted out together. "I want you, but I don't want to want you. We—"

He kisses me, cutting me off. My resistance melts at the shocking pleasure of Eli's mouth on mine. *I missed this.* His warm hand cradles my jaw as he deepens the kiss. I grip his shirt, keeping him close. *I need this.*

The kiss turns urgent. He lifts me to the counter, and I wrap my legs around him, my hands rapidly undoing the buttons on his shirt. His mouth shifts to my neck, and my fingers fumble as he gently bites the cord of my neck.

My breath stutters out. "Eli."

He lifts his head, our eyes meeting for a charged moment. I grab his head and kiss him again. There's nothing but heat and raw lust. It's heaven. Then he's lifting me, carrying me plastered against him to the bedroom.

The moment we get there, we strip. I grab a condom from the nightstand and hand it to him. No words. No false promises. Just what we both want.

Then I crawl onto the bed on all fours and wait for him.

He goes behind me. "Damn, that's a sexy sight." He enters me in a slow slide, pressing deep. I moan softly. Eli's powerful hands grip my hips, and then he thrusts faster and faster, pounding into me. I'm on fire, panting, my insides coiling tight.

He reaches one hand around to stroke pleasure central. There's nothing but sensation, the overwhelming strength and heat of him, unending pleasure. *Close, so close.* He seems to know, holding me back every time I get close, gentling his touch, and then pushing me right back to the edge.

His voice is harsh by my ear. "Ask me nicely."

"Please, please, please," I chant mindlessly.

He takes me all the way. I break, my body shuddering with pleasure, lost in it. I would collapse if he weren't holding me so tightly. My limbs feel weak, all of me overheated and shaky.

"More," he demands.

He strokes gently, taking me slow and deep for a neverending pleasure ride. I whimper incoherently, trembling with all that he makes me feel. The pressure builds, white-hot sensations flooding me. My release hits hard, and I cry out with the explosion of pleasure. He rides it out with me, drawing out more shockwaves of pleasure before letting go, clutching me tightly against him.

My head drops to the pillow, my cheek hitting the cool silk.

He brushes the hair out of my face. "You okay?"

"Good," I manage.

He pulls out, and I collapse to the mattress. I hear him padding away, going into the en suite bathroom. I'm limp and oddly happy. How can I be happy with all the turmoil I have going on?

Ugh, what am I doing? We broke up. I shouldn't be hooking up with him again. That sends the wrong message.

I'm nearly asleep when the covers lift and Eli gets into bed with me. His skin is bare and warm, pressing up next to me. He turns off the light on the nightstand.

Wake up!

I roll to my back and turn on the light on the nightstand. Then I stare at the ceiling, unable to make direct eye contact. "I shouldn't have done this to you. I seduced you, and that was wrong."

He covers my body, resting his weight on his forearms. "I seem to remember me doing this to you." His finger trails across my collarbone, sending tingles everywhere he touches. "I made you shudder under me, making sexy, throaty cries of passion. I seem to remember some begging too."

I shove his shoulder, my gaze fixed on his chin. "Please don't make this difficult. We broke up. This is the last time, okay?"

I risk a look at him. His warm hazel eyes, square clean-shaven jaw, his thick corded neck. A fresh rush of desire surprises me. I'm usually done with the lusting part afterward.

He gives me a slow, sexy smile like he knows what I'm thinking. He dips his head, nuzzling into my neck. My hand goes to his chest, intending to push him away, but I can't seem to find the willpower. Intense desire rockets through me. My legs open under him, a delicious ache deep inside drawing me back, making me greedy for more. His hand slides down my side, over my hip, and to the inside of my thigh. Sparks fire over my skin everywhere he touches.

He kisses me tenderly and then lifts his head to gaze into my eyes. I suddenly want to turn off the light. It's too intimate, the way he gazes, the tenderness. I reach blindly for the light but can't make contact.

I push at his shoulders frantically. "This is wrong. We shouldn't have done this."

He grabs my wrists and pins them to the mattress. "Be a little naughty."

My breath comes harder. I hate to admit it, but I'm excited by his grip on me. "We broke up. We should stop, pretend this never happened."

He slowly lowers his head, never breaking eye contact. His words run hot over my lips. "Not yet."

His kiss is gentle, his grip on my wrists firm, and I surrender to bliss.

13

Jenna

The next day I zip across the street to the Summerdale library as soon as I close up shop at four. Audrey works until five on Sunday, and I desperately need to confess or I'll burst. Eli went off to work early this morning, and I went to work shortly afterward in a complete fog. I can't stop thinking about my night with Eli, and I need to stop because it can never happen again. I need a sympathetic ear, who won't judge me for letting lust and longing get the better of me.

The library is a modern angular building with gray clapboard siding. The height of 1969 modern, that is. More recently, they added skylights, a large loft space, and a brand-new children's room on the side that nearly doubled the space. The automatic glass front door slides open as I approach, and I walk in to the brightly lit space. The faint smell of books lingers in the air.

Audrey's behind the front desk, helping check out books along with one of her part-time workers.

I wave to Audrey, and she smiles and waves back. Her smile drops as Drew appears from the second-story loft, carrying a thick book as he strides to the front desk. He's normally the definition of badass, a blackbelt running his own dojo and a former Army Ranger, but there's something about his expression that looks vulnerable. Hmm…I've never seen him in the library before.

He waits in Audrey's line to check out his book. Audrey looks around the older man she's helping toward Drew. "You can go over to Suzanne," she says, gesturing him over.

"I'm good here," he says.

I shift to the edge of the counter, staying far enough away so it's not obvious I'm eavesdropping.

Audrey's cheeks are flushed pink as she checks out a large stack of mysteries. Finally, it's Drew's turn, and he slides over his thick book without a word. It's a biography on Eisenhower, probably six hundred pages. Heavy reading.

She stares at the book for a moment before lifting her head. "Do you have a library card?"

"I used to. I can't find it."

Audrey nods. "Suzanne will get you set up. I need to—"

"Wait." He leans across the counter, speaking in a low voice. Dammit. I can't make out what he's saying.

Her lips part.

He straightens and looks at her expectantly.

She tucks her long black hair behind her ears. "Sure. Okay."

"So…"

She smiles tightly. "I'll see you around, okay?"

His face falls. "Yeah, okay." He catches my eye before swiftly turning away and walking toward the door.

"You forgot your book!" Audrey calls after him.

He lifts a hand. "Another time."

He wasn't here for the book.

Audrey gestures for me to follow her to her office. We go up the four stairs to the loft, where her office is in back. She shuts the door behind us and immediately removes her gray cardigan. Now she's in a cream blouse buttoned to the top. She always looks so professional at work, even though it's just regular old townspeople here. It's not like it's a corporate job.

She sits in a maroon cushioned office chair at her desk,

and I take the black cushioned smaller chair across from her. "What's up?" she asks. "Your text was so cryptic."

"Are you okay?"

"Yes, I'm fine. What's going on with you?"

I cross my legs and then uncross them. Then I check out my cuticles. I came here to confess, and suddenly I don't want to share. It's just so…wrong what I did. Maybe if I pretend it never happened, no one will ever have to know, and things will go back to normal. Relatively normal. This whole experience with Eli has been surreal from start to finish. And start again. Are we still involved?

I never would've let things move forward if I hadn't known deep down that he's a good guy from a good family. There's a basic level of trust there. Does that mean I made a mistake ending it? Or that I made a mistake sleeping with him again? What do I do? I've never been in such a strange situation before. I'm so confused I don't even know where to begin, so instead I focus on Audrey's unusual visitor.

"What was that about with Drew?"

She twirls a lock of her hair. "He just wanted to check out a book." Lie. That's her tell; twirling her hair gives her comfort over her little white lie.

"What did he say when he leaned across the counter?"

She blows out a breath. "He just asked if we could be friends again and maybe hang out sometime."

"Omigod, Aud, that's huge! I don't think you ever hung out with him before. You never know—"

"I know," she says flatly. "I agreed just to be polite. Look, I've thought long and hard about this, and the fact is he will always see me as the lovestruck middle-school girl I was when I wrote him during his deployments. I'm sure I sounded gushing and enthusiastic in those emails, but my feelings were real, even at thirteen."

"I know they were." We spent endless hours talking about them.

Her lips press into a flat line. "He'll never take me seriously."

"I think he misses your adoration. He even pretended to

want to read a book on Eisenhower. Blech." I stick out my tongue in disgust.

She laughs mirthlessly. "Yeah. Even if he did take the book home, I doubt he'd even make it past chapter one. He's not a big reader. I'm not sure why I ever thought we'd be compatible. You know me. Books are my life."

"Okay, so maybe he's never going to be a reader. Then why did he show up here today? Or does he usually pop in for a visit, and you never shared it with me?" I put on a mock angry face.

"No, that was the first time he visited." She sighs. "Maybe you're right. He missed my adoration. He knows I've moved on, and maybe it bugs him that I'm not that wide-eyed schoolgirl with a mad crush on him. He lost his little fan club."

"Have you moved on?" I ask gently.

She lifts her chin. "I signed up for eLoveMatch, didn't I?"

"Yes, but you stopped accepting dates and deleted your profile."

She slashes a hand through the air. "A temporary break. I'm still hopeful for a serious relationship soon. I want that, Jenna. I'm twenty-nine, and I'm more than ready for marriage and kids. I've always wanted to be a mom."

My chest aches in sympathy, and I reach across the desk to give her hand a squeeze. I'm starting to understand that longing for kids, it's visceral. Biology at work. The sad thing is, she hasn't even made it past a first date with a guy in more than a year. It's not looking good for her dream.

I release her hand, take a deep breath, and whisper, "I need to tell you something, and you can't tell Syd. I slept with Eli again last night. I told him that was the last time. I don't know what came over me."

Her eyes gleam. "The sex must be great if he tempted you after you ended it."

"Now I don't know if I made a mistake ending it, or by sleeping with him again."

"He's a good guy, and you're awesome. I still don't understand why you ended it in the first place."

"I told you because we want different things. That's exactly why Sydney didn't want me with him. You know how she gets about him and Caleb. She helped raise them."

"So what does Eli think about all this?"

I fidget, playing with some paperclips on her desk. "I don't know. He left for work this morning before I was fully awake. He just said he had to go to work and kissed me goodbye."

"And what did you say?"

"I was barely awake. I just said mmm-hmm."

She shoots me a pointed look. "What are you doing here talking to me? Go talk to him."

"Because I don't know the right thing to do. Maybe I shouldn't do anything. Just let it stand that we broke up and had this one last time together. I even told him that. I said this is the last time." *Right before we did it again.*

"Maybe you could just try dating again. You were really just in the beginning of…well, at the early stages of…"

My nerves stand on edge. "What? A relationship?"

"Yes, and I know you don't like that word—" she holds up a palm "—but in the beginning things are fragile. And that doesn't mean seeing him again has to be a heavy committed thing. It can be light and casual."

I shake my head. "He's not a light and casual kind of guy."

"Okay," she says slowly.

"He kidnapped me for our first date."

"True."

"He told me he's had a crush on me since he was a teen. He said I've always been his dream girl." I throw my hands up, knocking her paper clip holder to the floor. Paper clips go flying, along with the plastic cube. I turn to her in complete exasperation. "How am I supposed to live up to that?"

She stares at me, her mouth opening and closing again. Her brows furrow for a moment. Is it that hard to understand? Or maybe she's thinking of how Drew was *her* dream guy. Maybe he feels like he could never live up to that too.

We stand at the same time to clean up the mess.

"I got it, Aud."

She looks down at me as I clean up. "I admit dream girl sounds like a lot to live up to, but why don't you let him get to know you well enough to see if you live up to the hype? As I'm sure you will."

I continue picking up paper clips. "Don't you see that's just a mess of hurt feelings either way?" I stand and deposit the paper clip holder on her desk. "If I live up to the hype initially, it won't last because I can't give him that pretty domestic scene he wants. And if I don't, he's disappointed and hurt too."

She takes her seat again. "He said he wants a pretty domestic scene?"

I sit too. "Syd mentioned it, and I can read between the lines with him."

"Your parents are not you," she says quietly. "You're perfectly capable of settling down with someone you love."

My brows shoot up. "It was horrific. I'm never going through that, and I'm never putting any kids through that." I square my shoulders and straighten my spine. "I'm perfectly happy with my life just the way it is."

"Have you seen how happy Sydney is now that she's married? She practically floats through her day."

"Sydney was always going to get married. Her parents were happy together. She always said they were inseparable right from the start. Her dad proposed on their *first date.* That's not where I come from."

"But that *is* where Eli came from. He could be the kind who sticks if you gave him a chance, and then Sydney would have to be okay with you guys. Everything would work out perfectly. You and Eli could both stick and be happy together. I don't think we'd be talking so much about him if you didn't have some feeling for him."

She's completely missing the point!

I stand abruptly. "You don't understand. Forget I said anything."

She stands. "Come on, don't go. I'm not trying to piss you off. I want you to be happy."

"I am!"

I clench my jaw and walk out the door. Audrey is projecting her own longing for a serious relationship onto me. Doesn't she see? I did the wrong thing, again, and I need to find a way to move past it before Sydney figures out just how much I screwed up.

I'm not calling Eli because that would only imply I want more. I ended it; I never should've been with him again. That's the last time. I know when to stop.

~

Eli

I'm not chasing Jenna. The morning after our hookup, I left for my early shift at work and gave her a kiss goodbye. No sweet words. No promises. She has to meet me halfway.

Only she doesn't.

It's now been four days. After my usual morning workout in my home gym, I shower and flop down on the living room sofa. I don't know why this is bugging me so much. We had a good time. I should just be happy with what we had—temporary pleasure between two people who broke up. What guy wouldn't like that easy pleasure?

Me. I don't like it.

I leap off the sofa. I have too much restless energy, and I don't have work until tonight. I need to go for a run and not think about Jenna.

I lace up my sneakers. My schedule changes according to the chief's schedule. When I'm chief, I'll hire someone to work around *my* schedule.

I go for a long run with Lucy, shower, and flop down on my sofa again. Caleb's out, meeting up with some friends in the city. The house feels eerily quiet. Lucy lies at my feet, tuckered out from our run. I let out a breath. I don't know how I still have all this energy.

It's not quite lunchtime, but what the hell. I look at Lucy. "There's nothing that says I can't stop at Summerdale Sweets for a snack just like any other citizen, right?"

Lucy cocks her head and answers in the affirmative with her throaty incomprehensible sounds.

Good enough. I take her out for a pee break, retrieve her rubber figure-eight chew toy, and set it at her feet. If I'm gone too long, she'll chew, so I always leave her with an acceptable chew thing. She's much better now that she's thirteen months. Her puppy teething was a nightmare for my shoes, remote controls, and, once, a throw pillow.

I make the short drive to the bakery. I don't see any customers inside. I get out of the Mustang and resist running my fingers through my hair. It's not my hair that's the problem. I'm not exactly sure what is—too much history on my part, too much baggage on her part—all I know is that there's something special between us. I'm experienced enough to know that much.

I lean down to the driver's side mirror and check my look. I'm *not* chasing. This is a friendly visit. After all, we're bound to run into each other at some point. We live in the same small town and know a lot of the same people. Never mind that I managed to avoid her for a year.

I stride toward the door and open it. The bell jingles, announcing my arrival. I stop just inside the door, momentarily frozen as our eyes meet. She's so beautiful. Tall and slender, her blond hair just brushing her shoulders. Her apron is tied snugly, emphasizing her narrow waist. The blood rushes through my veins.

"Eli," she says softly.

"Hi, I was just out for a run, and your shop was on my route." She should know I'm not chasing her. I legitimately worked up an appetite.

"Don't need an excuse to treat yourself," she says brightly. "What can I get you?"

Right. I step closer, feigning interest in the glass case of baked goods. "What do you recommend?"

"You might like the peanut butter cookies. They're not super sweet."

Her tone is bland, her expression neutral. *Is she covering up real feeling for me, or does she just want me to leave?*

A chime goes off, and she turns, heading toward the back door of her shop. A delivery guy wearing a brown uniform steps inside with two large boxes. He's in his twenties, dark skin, buff with muscle. His slow smile aimed at Jenna tells me he's into her. His husky voice confirms it. "Hey, Jenna, got your delivery."

"You know where to put it, Trey," she responds in a flirty voice full of innuendo.

Jealousy spikes through me, and I never get jealous. I turn away, embarrassed over it. I don't have a claim to her. Not anymore.

He chuckles low and goes to a room in the back of the shop.

Jenna follows him, standing in the doorway, flirting some more. I can't make out what they're saying, but her hand's on her hip.

Trey brushes past her in the doorway, his dark eyes smoldering down at her. "Until next time." He must sense my glare because our eyes meet while he says to her, "Looks like you have a hungry customer. Maybe you should see what he wants."

Jenna dismisses it airily. "Just a friend."

Trey smirks at me and leaves.

My jaw clenches. *Just a friend? I don't think so!* "Were you with him?"

She goes back to the counter. "None of your business. So did you decide what you want?"

I want you.

"He wants you," I say.

She gestures toward the back door where he just left. "Trey's a nice guy. Smart too. He's going to night school for his MBA. He's actually on the management track at his work, but they make managers work every role so they understand the business."

"I'm smart."

She lifts her palms. "Okay, Eli, it's not a competition."

"I'm going to be police chief when Chief Daniels retires."

"Glad to hear it. Really."

The spike of jealousy turns into irrational anger. "I don't want you having sex with him."

She rolls her eyes. "We already did, and it's over. He's cool with it."

I jab a hand in the air. "Then why is he flirting with you like he wants you again?"

She shrugs. "Probably because he does, but he respects what I told him. Why are you really here? I hope you didn't get the wrong idea after—"

"Where did you hook up with him? Here in the shop?" I need to know. This guy shows up regularly with deliveries and his innuendo and smoldering good looks. Not cool.

She crosses her arms. "I'm not having this conversation with you."

I go behind the counter and look around in the back of the shop.

"Excuse me?" she says, her voice reaching a high note. "What are you doing?"

I peer into the room where he just dropped off boxes. It's a large storeroom with industrial shelves lining two walls. "It was in here, wasn't it?"

She stands in the doorway and glares at me. "Yes. Happy now?"

"And you never even came close to a repeat performance?" I get the feeling if I weren't here, something easily could've happened. He's an obvious flirt, and she reciprocated.

"We agreed up front it would be a onetime thing." She jabs me in the chest. "Not that it's your business."

I grab the wrist of her jabbing hand, and her face flushes, her lips parting. She wants me. "You never told *me* it was a onetime thing."

She pulls her wrist free. "You're right. Maybe I should have."

I step closer. "But you can't just pretend it wasn't phenomenal between us. You're experienced enough to know it's not always like that."

She's quiet, her eyes wary.

"We have something," I say, careful not to admit too much. I hate that it feels so one-sided.

"What?"

"You tell me."

She searches my expression before finally saying, "Passion."

"And a long history. I'm not the delivery guy you just met."

She throws her hands up. "No kidding! That's why it's extra important to keep boundaries between us. And that's also why I broke up with you, so no one gets hurt."

I lower my voice as the truth finally sinks in. "But that's not what you said. You said we had to break up because we wanted different things. The truth is, you're terrified of feeling anything. You don't let anyone in close."

She looks away. "That's not true. I'm close to Audrey, Sydney, Harper. Lots of people."

"You're only close with the people you've known since you were a kid. Well, guess what? You've known me that long too."

Her eyes flash. "It's different, and you know it. You have expectations I could never live up to."

I step into her space and brush a lock of hair behind her ear. "Tell me you feel nothing for me, and I'll walk away."

Her breath hitches. A long moment passes, our gazes locked. "I feel nothing for you." She sounds defeated.

"Liar. Stop letting your fear stand in the way."

"I'm not!"

"Prove it."

She grabs my head and kisses me, exactly as I knew she would. Proving herself. Jenna never could stand to look weak. I take over the kiss, my fingers gripping her hair, demanding everything. The fire burns between us. I shut and lock the door behind us and pin her against it.

She yanks at my clothes, needing me as much as I need her. I let her strip me down, and then I turn her, untying her apron and taking it off. I turn her back to me, pulling her shirt over her head.

"Condoms are on the top shelf," she says, yanking her jeans and panties off.

I look to a plain white box on the top shelf. "How many guys do you take back here?"

"Just Trey. I put a strip up there, not because I thought we'd go more than once, just because that's what I grabbed."

My chest tightens. I reach up, grab one, and roll it on. "No more. This is you and me. Your last memory of a hard fuck in the storeroom."

I hitch her leg up and press at her entrance. "Tell Trey you're seeing someone next time he's here."

Her head drops back. "I doubt he'll ask. Stop teasing me and do it."

I lift her against the door. "Wrap your legs around me." As soon as she does, I thrust hard. I hear her sharp intake of breath.

I hold her jaw, my voice fierce. "Think about us. Just us. Right here, right now."

Her lips part. "You're very sexy when you get aggressive."

I grind against her, and her eyes roll back in her head. The thin line of control snaps. I pound into her. She throws her head back, her nails digging into my shoulders, as I stake my claim.

"This is right," I tell her. "Us."

Her answer is a breathy, "Yes."

I slide a hand between us, stroking her. She bucks wildly. "Eli!"

"Yes, say my name."

She chants it as I take her hard and fierce, my fingers working her. Her body contracts around me, and then she lets go, shuddering with her release. I pump again and again before my own release roars through me.

I lean heavily against her, our bodies heated, my limbs weak from the rush. I carefully lift her off me and set her on her feet.

We stare at each other.

"I missed you," she says softly, and then she kisses me. A sweet kiss that nearly brings me to my knees.

I wrap my arms around her, speaking near her ear. "I missed you too."

She hugs me tight and burrows into my chest. "I told myself it was a mistake to hook up with you after we broke up, but I can't seem to resist you."

"Then don't. Stop fighting it. We'll both be so much happier."

She looks up at me, her green eyes shining with what looks like love. "It was a mistake to break up with you. I regret it. I'm so sor—"

"Shh, you don't have to be sorry. It's done, and now we move past it. Together."

She peppers kisses all over my face. "Thank you for being so understanding. I never wanted to hurt you."

"I know."

She hugs me again, and I hold her head against me, letting out a breath of relief. She met me halfway. She missed me as much as I missed her.

She lifts her head. "We have to hide it from Sydney because beginnings are fragile. This is our beginning."

"No, we can't hide this. That's only going to hurt her. Either you tell her or I will."

Her eyes are beseeching. "Eli, please."

"No."

She runs her fingers through my hair. "I need time. It's my first real relationship, and I'm not ready for harsh judgment on it. Even Audrey said I should protect the relationship in the beginning because it's a delicate fragile thing."

That soft spot I've always had for Jenna seals the deal. "Okay, but we're not a secret for too long."

14

Jenna

More than two weeks pass in utter bliss. Eli is above and beyond any expectations I ever had about relationships. He brings me flowers for no good reason, texts me he's thinking about me, and he's affectionate just because, not as foreplay. I even asked him if he was like this with every relationship he has, and he told me that was a ridiculous question because he's never been in a relationship with me before. I'm beginning to think I love him. I keep it to myself though, not even sharing with Audrey. Eli's been more adamant that we need to tell Sydney, but I've held him off. I'm not ready to let anything make this happy bubble burst. I've never felt this way before. I practically float through my days.

I'm on my lunch break at work, checking my email, when harsh reality intrudes in the form of an invitation to my parents' Halloween-themed wedding in two weeks. Bile rises in my throat. Do they see the irony of a spooky scary holiday for their second wedding to each other? I don't respond. Obviously, I don't want to go, but I'm postponing a reply because then Mom and probably Dad will want to talk to me about it.

There's another email from Eve Larsen. I gasp. I haven't

heard from my sister in years. I guess she dropped the nickname Evie. I tap on the email with a shaking finger.

Hi Jenna, it's been way too long between sisters. For a long time I felt like we had to take sides, and you had chosen the opposite of me. I'll be honest, I've had some difficulties over the years that have prevented me from having good relationships in my life. All this stuff with our parents made me realize if they can forgive each other, surely you and I can make up. Or at least talk. Will you be at their wedding? I'd like to have a chance to talk face-to-face.

I'm in California now, so it's not as easy to meet up. I hope to see you there.

Eve

I let out a breath. The one hurt from my past that was worse than missing my dad or losing my beloved dog was the loss of my little sister. Now I feel like I have to go to the wedding.

I call Mom. "I got the invitation. I just want you to know I'll be there. I don't pretend to understand—"

"Jenna, your dad and I married so young the first time. I dropped out of college to have you at eighteen, and he dropped out to get a job to support us both. It was hard. We didn't have the support of our parents. We were doing the best we could."

"You were so angry with each other for so long."

She sighs. "We were still learning who we were as people, and we were struggling. I'd like to think that we've both matured. Time and distance have made us realize that what drew us to each other in the beginning is still there."

"You met at a kegger. I'm sure beer goggles helped."

"I understand your anger. Things got out of hand during the divorce."

I jam a hand in my hair. "You think?"

"I'm sorry, Jenna. Truly. Your dad is too. That's why we've

been trying to talk to you. Maybe we can all sit down for dinner—"

Nausea roils through my gut. "No, that's okay. I'll see you at the wedding. I gotta go. I'm at work."

I say bye and immediately call Eli.

"Hello," he says warmly. "I was just thinking about you."

My shoulders relax, and the nausea instantly settles. "You were?"

"Yup. Those crepes you made for breakfast with the apples and whipped cream were amazing."

I laugh. "Okay, so you love my skills in the kitchen."

"More than that, beautiful."

My heart races as it hits me—I love him. I love hearing his voice, love his smile, just plain love being with him, both in bed and out. I'm suddenly tongue-tied.

"You okay?" he asks.

"Yes, sorry. Flailing a bit here over an email I just got. I have a favor to ask, and I totally understand if you don't want to do it."

"Ask away."

"My parents are getting remarried in two weeks. Halloween-themed wedding. I know it sounds hideous. I wasn't going to go, but then my sister, Evie, well, she's Eve now, asked me to. She wants to reconnect."

"I remember Evie. We were in the same grade. Serious kid."

"Yeah, I guess. Neither of us are sunshine and roses."

"You're roses. Elegant and classy."

My cheeks flush at the compliment. "Eli."

"Are you blushing?"

"No. Stop."

"Yeah, you are. Okay, I'll go and help you face down the horror show."

He really gets it. What a great guy! "Thank you."

"You'll owe me a huge favor though."

I can hear the smile in his voice. "Oh yeah? What's that?"

"I'll let you know when the next obligatory social function

pops up, and you'll so be there. High school reunion? Ex's wedding? Family dinner?"

"Oh, come on, you have a great family."

"They're relentless."

"So are you."

He lets out a manly sigh. "You love it."

I smile. "You have your moments."

"Actually, a family dinner would be a good idea, bring this out in the open and come clean with Syd."

I stop smiling. "No."

His voice turns coaxing. "We've been seeing each other for more than six weeks now."

A tickling of unease goes through me. "No, it's been, like, two weeks."

"Two weeks since the breakup hiccup. Before that we went to New Hampshire, and we spent time together, circling the attraction, both of us into each other. You admitted you've been lusting for me since you bumped into my car and got the full Eli effect up close and personal."

I pace the hallway in the back of my shop. "I guess I didn't realize how long it's been."

"August thirty-first we had our first lunch together. It's now the middle of October."

"That was just lunch to work out the accident finances."

"Jenna, this thing between us is not that fragile, I promise you."

I flush. His warm confident voice does something to me, setting my stomach aflutter, all of me lighting up. Still, it feels too soon to go public. "Okay, I get it. We've kinda sorta been seeing each other for six weeks, but if you count the official date as when—"

"You watched me play guitar like a groupie."

"When you kidnapped me."

He chuckles. "The fact is, this has been going on too long to hide it. If you can bring me to a family function, then I can bring you to one. That's what serious couples do."

"What do you mean by serious?" My voice sounds high and reedy.

"I mean it's time to stop pretending this is just uncontrollable lust on both of our parts. It's mutual adoration. I'll set up dinner."

I don't even have a moment to bask in the mutual adoration comment with the threat of a family dinner. "No, wait! Can we do it after my parents' wedding? I just need a little more time."

"No. That's two weeks away. We'll do it this weekend."

"Syd always works weekends."

"Then I'll find out when she's available, and we'll all sit down together and explain what's what. No more secrets."

Maybe he's right. I just can't shake the feeling that Sydney will be furious with me both for hiding it and for being with the one guy she told me to stay away from. But he's impossible to resist, and I do have feelings for him. Real deep feelings.

"I completely understand what you're saying about not hiding things from Sydney," I say. "I'd like to tell her myself one-on-one, okay? No witnesses."

"That works too. Once you do, then we'll do a family dinner. I'm sure everything will go smoothly. She loves you."

"Yeah." *She just doesn't love me for her younger brother.*

"See you tonight," he says and hangs up.

I let out a shaky sigh and go back to work.

~

Eli

I head into work the next night for my late shift in a good mood. Things are going great with Jenna, and she finally agreed to tell Sydney this Thursday at ladies' night. I let myself into the small police station in a former two-story Victorian house. I spot Chief Daniels in his office, the door open.

"Hey, Chief."

"Eli, come into my office."

"Yes, sir."

"Have a seat," he says jovially. He's not a real cheerful

guy, which gives me hope. Maybe he's finally decided to retire. He's gone back and forth on the date for more than a year.

I take the hard wooden chair across from his cushy full-size desk chair. That's basically how it's been since I started. He's the chief, so he gets the comfortable choice of chairs, schedule, and bigger salary. I'm the underling, so I get night shift and the tough stuff he doesn't want to deal with in the community—naked sunbathers, raccoons in the garbage, kids drinking beer on the roof of the high school, etc. He'd be lost without me.

"Big news," he says. "I'm retiring at the end of the year."

I stifle a cheer, but I can't help my smile. "Congratulations!" I wait for the part that's most important to me.

"As of New Year's Day, you are officially the new chief of police."

My shoulders pull back, chest puffed with pride. "Thank you, I appreciate your faith in me."

"And congratulations to you. Son, I couldn't be happier leaving Summerdale in your capable hands. Feel free to hire another you. Might be hard to find someone for January, but give it a try. If needed, we could hire part-timers on a rotating basis from neighboring towns."

My limbs feel light, and I find myself smiling, my new title rolling around in my mind—Chief Robinson. "I'll put some feelers out for my replacement."

He folds his hands behind his head and leans back in his seat. "I'm off to sunny Florida."

Just like all the old people in town I think but don't say. It's a popular retirement destination and only a three-hour plane ride away. "Good for you."

"Yup. Living the dream, and Martha is looking forward to it as well. She's the one who pushed me to go. I'm not getting any younger." He chuckles, looking happier than I've ever seen him. "You'll be getting a pay bump and an extra week of vacation." He slides some paperwork over to me. "Take a look and, if you're happy with the terms, go ahead and sign off on them."

He stands, walks around the desk, and claps a hand on my shoulder. "Chief Robinson. Has a nice ring to it, doesn't it?"

I smile. "Sure does. Thank you, sir."

He nods and heads out the door.

I look over the contract, sign it, and leave it in his top desk drawer. I look around, bouncing on the balls of my feet. I'm in a good place in my life now—career set, pay bump, dream girl. I can see a future with Jenna here in Summerdale like a dream on the horizon. I just hope she's on board.

~

"What do you mean you didn't tell Sydney?" I ask under my breath. We're standing behind rows of metal folding chairs for Jenna's parents' outdoor wedding. We showed up a little early so she'd have time to talk to her sister, Evie, before the ceremony. Most of the guests have arrived already, except Evie.

"We'll talk about it later," Jenna says, wringing her hands together and looking around.

I'm pissed. Jenna didn't tell Sydney about us last Thursday at ladies' night because Sydney was mad about some issue with a supplier, and Jenna didn't think it was the right time. She swore she'd do it this week. Now I find out it still didn't happen. I can read between the lines—Jenna's not serious about us. And here I am imagining a rosy future together. Someone serious wouldn't keep our relationship from their closest friend. I'm tired of sneaking around.

I'm about to say that when she says, "I feel like I'm going to throw up."

I rub her back. "Okay, just take a deep breath. Evie wants to see you. This is good."

She grips my hand; hers is ice cold. I back off the whole Sydney thing. Jenna's having a hard enough time going to her parents' wedding and reuniting with her sister for the first time in years.

I don't know Jenna's parents very well. I was nine when

they split up. Her mom worked full time for a computer company. I remember she was blonde and thin like Jenna. I know even less about her dad, but here we are at their wedding. It's at a historic farmstead with a small lattice canopy draped with fake fall leaves and cobwebs for the ceremony, as well as a black aisle runner. Just beyond the ceremony area is a large old barn with weathered gray siding, the doors wide open. Inside, the barn is filled with tables and flowers for the reception.

Jenna crushes my hand. "I think that's her. Evie."

Her sister's hair is dirty blond, cut just at her jawline, emphasizing the sharp lines of her face. Just like Jenna, she's tall, both of them wearing a black sleeveless dress. Evie's brows lift, an uncertain expression on her face as she approaches us. "Jenna?"

Jenna nods and pulls me with her to meet her sister halfway. "Yes. Hi, Evie."

"It's just Eve now."

Jenna nods again, and we stop, standing on a grassy spot a short distance from the ceremony area. "Yes. Sorry. How are you? What brought you all the way out to California?"

She glances at me. "I'm good. I work in TV as a writer on *Irreverent*."

"Really? That's amazing. I've seen it a few times. I had no idea."

Eve ducks her head, smiling. "Yeah, most people don't pay attention to the writer credits."

Jenna lets go of my hand and lifts her arms in the air almost like she wants to hug her sister. "Well, congratulations!"

"Thanks. It took a while, but I'm happy with where I'm at. I'd like to sell my feature-length screenplays too. It's a long shot. TV needs more people." She looks up at me and squints. "Why do you look so familiar?"

I offer my hand. "Eli Robinson. We were in the same grade at Summerdale Elementary."

She gasps. "Look at you, all grown up! I remember you were always getting into trouble."

"And now I'm a cop."

She looks between me and Jenna. "Wow. I'm blown away. Eli Robinson is a cop, and you're with Jenna." She turns to Jenna. "And what do you do?"

Jenna smiles. "I own my own bakery, Summerdale Sweets."

Eve tilts her head. "That's a surprise too. I remember you were good at math and science. I couldn't relate as a kid."

Jenna nods. I don't think I've ever seen her nod so much. "I worked in IT for a while—computer network systems—until I burned out. I feel good when I bake, and I like bringing that joy to people. It makes them happy to go home with a special treat."

"Sure, sure," Eve says.

An awkward silence falls while they look around at our surroundings. We're in a clearing with trees edging the property in the distance. There's a few hay bales with scarecrows and pumpkins set up.

"You think the bride will dress in costume?" I ask.

Jenna and Eve laugh.

"I assume so," Eve says.

"I'd be disappointed if she didn't," Jenna says.

"Have you talked to Mom recently?" Eve asks.

"No," Jenna says. "Have you talked to Dad?"

"Only to tell him I'd be here."

"Honestly, I'm still not cool with the remarriage after everything they put us through. I'm only here for you."

"Can I hug you?" Eve asks uncertainly.

"Of course!" Jenna exclaims, throwing her arms around her younger sister.

I rub my eye. Some dust caught in there.

Jenna sniffles and rubs her eye too. "I've missed you, Eve. I feel like we lost so much time because of our parents' garbage."

"I missed you too." She lowers her voice. "I was in a bad place for a long time, struggling with addiction. I'm clean now, and I'm trying to make amends with the people in my life who mean something special. Like you."

They both turn at a man wearing a dark gray suit. His blond and white hair is slicked back.

"Hi, Dad," Eve says.

Jenna lifts a hand in a small wave.

Mr. Larsen is jovial. "Hi, everyone, thanks for coming to our special day." He hugs Eve and looks toward Jenna.

Jenna gives him a quick hug but seems stiff. "You remember Eli."

He gives me a hearty handshake. "Sure, good to see you again."

"You too. Congratulations."

He beams. "Thanks."

"No costume?" Eve asks him.

He rubs his hands down the front of his blazer. "I was overruled. Halloween theme is strictly for decorations. Though we do plan on visiting Salem, Massachusetts, for our second honeymoon, where they had the Salem witch trials." He takes a deep breath and looks around. "I never thought this day would come."

"If only you'd never split up in the first place," Jenna mutters.

Her dad gets serious. "We were young and struggling the first time around, taking things out on each other. We're in a better place now. I'll see you at the reception. I'm going to say hello to a few people."

As soon as he's out of hearing range, Jenna says, "So casual about ripping our family apart."

"They're basically what not to do," Eve says. "I still can't believe they got back together *and* want to make it official. I'm never getting married. And I say that even after years of therapy dealing with the fallout from their divorce."

She's surprisingly open about everything. She hasn't seen me or Jenna in years. We're practically strangers to her.

"Me either," Jenna says. "Half the time it ends badly. Not worth it."

I hate that Jenna sees her parents' troubles as the only way marriages go, so I offer my own parents' example. "Or it goes great, and then one of them dies."

They turn to me with twin looks of horror.

"That's morbid," Eve says.

"That was my parents. I thought we were talking about our parents' deals."

Jenna gives me a sideways hug. "Sorry about your parents."

I put an arm around her shoulders. "My dad never regretted marrying young because it gave him more time with her. He always said true love is worth any struggle."

Eve stares at me, looking thoughtful before turning to Jenna. "Do you think our parents have true love?"

"No," Jenna says. "I think they're two middle-aged people who're tired of being alone."

My dream girl is disturbingly pessimistic about love. "Such a romantic," I tease, even though I'm uneasy.

"You know me by now," Jenna says.

I tell myself she's just like that about her parents. With us, things are different. Right?

But she still won't tell Sydney about us. That does *not* bode well for our future. If we even have a future. I might've built this up in my mind into more than it actually is, colored by the embarrassing fact that I've wanted her for way too long.

Music blares from loudspeakers. It's "The Monster Mash," and a woman gestures for everyone to take their seats.

"Perfect," Jenna whispers. "A monster wedding."

15

Jenna

I'm sitting between Eve and Eli in the front row, our assigned seats, attempting to look pleasant instead of seething like I really am. Dad looks eager, standing up there with his best man, a middle-aged bald guy I don't know. There's no line of bridesmaids or groomsmen, just creepy Halloween music while we all sit here, waiting for the bride. Probably there's a matron of honor coming soon too.

Dad keeps peering down the aisle. It's a small wedding, maybe thirty people who look to be their friends. My relatives aren't here. Maybe my parents didn't think our family would want to celebrate with them after all the turmoil. They're not on good terms with their parents since Mom got pregnant with me. That's right, I was the family wrecker before I was even born.

A brunette woman in a dark green satin dress carrying a bouquet of white carnations approaches Dad. Probably the matron of honor. She looks around Mom's age. His brows draw together as they talk.

I glance at my sister looking so grown up and put together. She'll be in town until tomorrow night. I hope we can spend more time together after this.

I lean over and whisper in her ear, "Do you think Mom changed her mind?"

She whispers back, "You know her better than I do. Would she do that?"

"I have no idea. I don't pretend to understand her."

I watch as Dad looks more and more anxious. The crowd is getting louder, everybody wondering what the holdup is.

Finally, Mom shows up, wearing a pink cocktail dress and a tiara. She looks pretty and still has her trim figure. Even I have to admit you'd never guess she was forty-eight. She had me at nineteen. People always used to say we could pass as sisters when all I wanted was my real sister back.

The wedding march begins, and she starts down the aisle at a sedate pace, holding a small bouquet of pale roses, tulips, and autumn leaves. About halfway down, her gaze darts side to side, and then her pace picks up like she's in a hurry to get to Dad. Maybe she's uncomfortable being the center of attention. Their first wedding was a quick courthouse ceremony.

The music stops belatedly as someone hurries over to turn it off.

The minister begins. "Dearly beloved…"

Mom holds her hand up to silence him. "Excuse me, I need to talk to Andrew."

Uh-oh. I exchange a pointed look with Eve. This is not good.

Mom and Dad are whispering to each other. Within moments, Dad's getting louder and louder.

Eve and I exchange a resigned look. We know the precursor to a fight. I glance at Eli, who looks uneasy.

"I'm sorry!" Mom cries. "I can't marry you."

"Why?" Dad asks. "You said you loved me, and I never stopped loving you, Meghan."

Mom waves her hands around. "Marriage is a big deal. Forever. It's too much pressure. We can't screw it up again." She flees, running toward the old farmhouse, where she probably left her clothes.

Dad chases her.

Everyone stands to watch as he calls after her. They disappear inside the house. So much drama just like always.

"Holy shit," Eli mutters.

I cross my arms. "I knew it. Thank God I never got invested in this reunion."

"I suspected as much too," Eve says, "but on the off chance it worked out, I didn't want them upset that I ditched their wedding. Talk about awkward for future family events."

"Like we ever had family events in the first place!" I exclaim.

Eve gives me a sympathetic look. "We should. Just us two. Maybe you could visit me in LA."

I smile, my eyes watering, my throat tight. "I'd like that. At least we got each other out of all this garbage."

"Sorry, Jenna," Eli says.

"It's nothing more than I expected," I say.

His eyes meet mine, his voice gentle. "Still, it's shitty."

The current situation on top of all the past hurt finally proves too much, and I find myself crying. I turn to Eve, the only person in the world who lived through what I have. "They're not meant to be together, and I don't know why they can't just get over it and move on. Why do they have to keep dragging us into their drama?"

"Love can be a real messed-up thing," Eve says, rubbing my arm. "You want to talk? We can go back to my hotel room, hit up the mini bar, and vent."

I nod through my tears. "That sounds great." I turn to Eli. "I'm going to go with Eve. I'll see you later."

"Stop by my place tomorrow," he says. "I have the late shift at work tonight."

"I'm probably going to be with Eve." I squeeze Eve's arm. "We have a lot of catching up to do, and she leaves tomorrow night."

"Can we talk for a minute?" he asks.

"Sure." I wipe my eyes and follow him a distance away.

"I could be there for you too, you know," he says.

"Thanks but Eve gets it. We both lived through the war."

He clenches his jaw. "Jenna, I'm trying real hard to be

patient with you, but I can't help but think you're not serious about us."

My lips part in surprise. "What?"

He jabs a hand in the air. "You won't tell Sydney about us. You turn to a virtual stranger instead of me when you're upset. It's obvious we're in two different places."

My eyes widen. I'm taken aback by his anger. "She's my sister. Why're you being like this? I'm the one who's upset now. You're supposed to be comforting."

He backs up a step. "Hey, take as much time as you need. Don't worry about me."

"Eli, come on. I do care."

He narrows his eyes. "Then why're we still a secret, huh? You're hedging your bets that we'll end soon, and you'll never have to deal with telling Syd."

I chickened out, but I can't say that. I did plan to tell her once I got through the trauma of my parents' wedding. I can only take so much emotional upheaval in my life. I told Eli I wanted to wait until after the wedding to tell her, but he insisted. I couldn't risk losing her in the midst of dealing with everything else.

"It just wasn't the right time," I say lamely.

"This isn't working for me anymore. Bye, Jenna."

He turns and strides away. What the hell? Did we just break up during my parents' horrific breakup?

"Your timing sucks!" I yell.

He doesn't look back.

~

Eli

My chest feels hollow, like Jenna's walking around with my heart instead of me. I let my temper get the best of me yesterday, already worked up that Jenna kept us a secret for so long. She had two whole weeks to tell Sydney, and she didn't. I suspected the worst, and then I beat her to it, ending it. *Idiot move.*

The only reason I didn't cancel on tonight's costume party

is because I'm hoping Jenna's here. It's Halloween night, and I have off because I took the late shift for mischief night last night. Boy, were those little hoodlums sorry they ever thought of toilet papering and egging people's property. I was in no mood for bullshit last night.

I park my Mustang in Wyatt and Sydney's long driveway on the side of their large two-story house with gray clapboard siding. There's a matching gray lighthouse with a white top to the right of the house. One of the eccentricities of its former owner, who planted a landlocked lighthouse here. It's actually a water tower done up to look like a lighthouse.

I get out of the car and take a deep breath of cool air, glancing around at the parked cars. I don't see Jenna's car, but she could've shown up with Audrey.

Jenna spent last night and most of today with her sister and didn't respond to my text or call. If we could just talk this through, I'm sure we could work it out. I won't even press her to come clean with Syd. We'll just step outside for a private conversation, where I'll explain I don't want to end it. I have a chip on my shoulder because I wanted her from way back, but it's time to let go of that fantasy and deal with the reality that is a relationship with Jenna. Things are great between us, not perfect obviously, but still.

I ring the bell, nervous energy racing through my limbs.

Wyatt answers the door, holding his white shih tzu, Snowball, under one arm. Snowball's dressed in a bumblebee costume. She looks perturbed by the outfit, as she should be, wearing a black headband with big yellow pom-pom antennae. His pit bull mix, Rexie, stands at his side, wearing pink butterfly wings and an equally ridiculous headband with pink and purple antennae.

"No barking at your visitor, huh?" I ask the dogs. Usually it's a free-for-all at the front door.

Wyatt smirks, he's king of the smirkers this guy. His brown hair is tousled, his jaw scruffy. "They're tired out by all the guests, and before you comment on their girly costumes, Kayla dressed them." That's his youngest sister, a sweet cheerful woman now engaged to my older much more reserved brother Adam.

"Could've guess it."

"Where's your costume?" he asks.

"Where's yours?"

"In the kitchen."

I follow him into a modern kitchen with a huge granite island and professional-grade stainless steel appliances. Adam and Kayla are standing at the island, along with my sister, Sydney, Wyatt's two sisters, Brooke and Paige, and a few people from around town. No Jenna or Audrey.

Wyatt puts on a headband with devil horns. "I'm Satan. Ask your sister."

Sydney points to her own devil horns. Her long auburn hair is up in a high ponytail. "And I'm his she-devil. Eli, come on, it's a costume party. What are you supposed to be?"

Depressed.

I pull off my leather jacket to show off my white shirt with a bar code across it that reads Generic Halloween Costume. I pull this baby out whenever I'm required to be in costume.

"Lame!" Sydney proclaims. "And that's like the eighth time you've worn that on Halloween!"

"Never goes out of style," I say.

"I like it," Wyatt says. "Clever. Help yourself to a drink. There's more people in the family room. I think someone wants to set up a séance, and there's a palm reader too."

I wonder if Jenna's in there. She could be with Audrey, my ally.

"Thanks." I say hello to everyone as I move through the kitchen, looking for something I'd like to drink. Wyatt stocked pumpkin beer, sweet wine, and mulled cider. None of them appeal.

My older brother Adam puts a local IPA in my hand. He's tall and lean with short dark brown hair and a perpetually scruffy jaw. "There you go. I brought my own stuff."

"Thanks."

I pop it open, take a drink, and smile at Kayla. She's petite, full of energy, with brown hair and light brown eyes like her brother, Wyatt. "How's the wedding planning going?" I ask not because I'm so into weddings, but because Adam and Kayla are wearing matching Bride and Groom T-shirts. She's even wearing a veil. Clearly this is something she'd like to talk about.

Surprisingly, Adam answers, "Good." He even smiles when he says it. He was never much of a smiler before Kayla.

"Fantastic!" Kayla exclaims, and then proceeds to fill me in on every detail of their wedding from the ring bearer's cute pillow to the outfit she plans on wearing as they head out for their honeymoon in Hawaii.

"I had no idea so much work went into a wedding," I say.

"That's why I'm so glad to have Hailey by my side. That's my wedding planner in Clover Park." She squeezes Adam's arm. "Adam likes her too."

I furrow my brows in concentration. That name sounds familiar.

"Sure do," Adam says. "Mostly because having a wedding planner makes Kayla so happy."

Kayla squeezes him around the middle. "Oh, Adam, I love you."

"I love you too," he says gruffly.

I turn away from all the love declarations, and Sydney grabs my arm, pulling me over to Wyatt's sisters. "You remember Brooke and Paige."

"Yes, I said hi to them earlier."

Sydney smiles widely. "Well, Brooke here is single."

My shoulders slump, suddenly so tired. This never would've happened if Jenna had told Sydney about us, and now we're not even together.

Brooke, a brunette with long straight hair, suddenly turns bright red, looking anywhere but at me. Probably doesn't help that she's caught off guard wearing a fuzzy gray mouse costume with a painted-on nose and whiskers.

Her sister Paige, a woman like Sydney—tough and speaks her mind—hides a smile as she makes her escape to the other room without a word. At least Paige wore a less embarrassing doctor costume, complete with stethoscope. There's some dignity to that. Poor Brooke is being set up when she's a mouse with whiskers.

"I thought we weren't doing this tonight," Brooke whispers to Sydney.

"Can I talk to you for a minute, Syd?" I ask.

"Sure, don't go anywhere, Brooke. We'll be right back."

I pull her across the room to the adjoining dining area. "Do *not* set me up with Brooke."

"Why not? You're the same age, both single. She's very nice and smart too. She's had a bad run of things with guys, but she's looking for someone more serious. That could be you. And she's an architect. How cool is that?"

"First of all, I don't need my sister finding me dates."

"This is different. She's family. I really like her, and if you gave her a chance—"

"Syd, no. Just drop it."

"You're still single, right?"

I am now. "Yes, but it's not happening."

"Oh, come on. Just talk to her."

I set my beer down on the table with a thunk. "Listen very carefully. Do not set me up with Brooke or anyone. I just broke up with the love of my life, I feel like shit, and I don't *want* anyone else, okay?" My voice got loud at the end there. I can't help it.

Her jaw drops.

I continue, the words tumbling out. "And you know part of the reason I'm not with her is because you kept telling her what a bad person she was for me, incapable of having a relationship, when you should've been encouraging her to try to get over her issues and give love a chance."

She stares at me. "Are you talking about Jenna? *She's* the love of your life? Why am I just now hearing about this?"

"Because she was terrified you wouldn't approve."

She looks over my shoulder, her eyes narrowing. I follow her gaze. Jenna and Audrey just arrived.

I take a step forward. "Jenna."

She halts in the front entryway, staring at me. She didn't wear a costume either. Her face is pale, her eyes tired looking.

Sydney looks between us. Audrey, dressed like a witch, gives me a small smile and makes her way to the kitchen.

I stride over to Jenna. "Can we get a minute alone?"

Sydney pops up by my side. "Wait, hold up."

"Syd," I snap, "just give us a minute."

"She's the reason you feel so shitty you can't say two words to another woman?" Sydney asks me.

"Yes, and I'd like to have a minute to talk to her without—"

"How could you!" Sydney exclaims at Jenna.

Jenna holds her hands up. "We broke up."

"More like you dumped him! Just like I knew you would."

"No, Syd," I start.

Sydney cuts me off to lay into Jenna. "I can't believe you went behind my back like this! How long has this been going on?"

"Not that long," Jenna says, sending me an imploring look.

Two months. I'm not going to lie, so I say nothing.

"How long is not that long?" Sydney asks, looking between us.

"I-I—" Jenna's face crumples. "I'm sorry, okay?"

She turns and races toward the front door. I follow close behind her.

"What's going on?" Wyatt says from behind us.

Sydney replies loud enough to reach our ears. "Oh, nothing, just my best friend going behind my back with my brother, who I told her to stay away from months ago!"

I shut the front door behind us just as Jenna gives me the saddest most broken look I've ever seen. "It's over, Eli. Everything's over. I'm going home."

"We need to talk."

She holds up a palm. "I'm never going to be the dream girl you hoped for. Why do you think Sydney's so angry? You had it right in the first place. We should just say bye and go our separate ways."

"I was wrong."

Her expression shuts down. She turns and hurries to her car.

Dammit.

"You can't just leave!" I yell after her. "What about Audrey?"

What about us?

She doesn't turn around. "She'll get a ride home with someone else." She gets into her car and takes off, driving over the front lawn in her hurry to get away.

I jam my hands on my hips. If she can't see what a great thing we had, that's on her.

I drop my head. Except it hurts me just as much.

16

Jenna

It's only been two days since the nightmare costume party, three days since Eli and I broke up after my parents' botched wedding, and it's been awful. I can't sleep, I can barely eat. Sydney won't talk to me. She's mad that I went behind her back, and who could blame her? And for what? Eli ended it because he suspected I wasn't as serious as he was. I don't even know what that means. Marriage? Maybe after he heard my sister and I talking about how we never wanted to get married, he saw the future clearly and didn't like what he saw. God, I knew everything would end horribly. I just never thought I'd have so much regret.

It's Tuesday, my day off, and I can't seem to move off the sofa. I've got stuff I need to get done today. There's only one woman on earth who might understand my situation—Eve. We spent hours talking after our parents' botched wedding. We talked about old times and our different perspectives on what went down. I shared with her then about Eli breaking up with me. She's got a lot of hard-won wisdom after therapy. I call her. It's afternoon here, and I hope I'm catching her on her lunch break in California.

As soon as she answers, I blurt, "Am I catching you at a bad time?"

"Just having a quick lunch in my car. Sometimes I need alone time after the crowd in the writers' room. Not that I don't love every single one of them. Just, you know, introverting."

I smile a little. I'm an extrovert, so it's interesting to me how different two sisters can be. Same gene pool, living through the same messed-up childhood. Maybe our parents are too different from each other too. I definitely took after Mom more and, now that I think about it, Eve is more like Dad. "Did you ever wonder why Mom and Dad got together in college?"

"I'm guessing hormones plus alcohol equaled love. They did meet at a party."

"Yeah. I thought something like that too." I sigh. "Things are really messed up with Eli. We broke up, and I think he wanted to patch things up, but then my best friend, his sister Sydney, found out I went behind her back to see him, and now she won't talk to me. I feel like I lost them both." Hot tears sting my eyes, and my voice chokes. "And I miss them so much."

"Did you say something that can't be unsaid to either of them?"

"No, I don't think so. I bailed on Eli when he tried to talk to me because Sydney was so furious about us—"

"Why would she be?"

"She knows how damaged I am and didn't want me to hurt him. She's not wrong. I've never had a good relationship, and look how screwed up this one got."

"Jenna, some of the things you say make me think that maybe you feel like you're not enough."

"Yes!"

"I felt the same way for a very long time. It wouldn't hurt you to try therapy to deal with some of the past issues so they don't pop up in your current relationships."

I run a shaky hand through my hair. "I never thought I'd have a relationship like this, you know? I don't think I would've gotten so close if it weren't him. Eli felt safe somehow. I guess because we've known each other so long."

"Safe, huh? Most people would find that boring, but I have a feeling safe is exactly what you need."

"Oh, he's not boring. Not at all. Most times I just feel like I can relax around him."

"Let down your walls."

"A little bit. Not enough, though. I should've told him how I feel. I am serious about him. I love him." A weight lifts, and I sit up on the sofa. "I really do. I'm not sure what that means for the future, but I should at least tell him that much, right?"

"Sounds like you already know the right thing to do."

Easier said than done.

"What if it's not enough? What if he says so what? It's scary."

"Only one way to find out."

Nerves race through me at the thought. "I guess you're right."

"I hope after our marathon talking session this past weekend—" she coughs out *free therapy* "—you have some perspective on things. What went down when we were kids had nothing to do with us. Still doesn't. None of it was our fault."

I take a deep breath, trying to believe the words deep down, where the hurt lives.

"I know you can do this. You took a great risk leaving your IT career and starting over with your own business. That took strength and a leap of faith. Exactly what you need to get Eli back."

"What if it's too late?"

"Wouldn't you rather know for sure than do nothing?"

"When you put it that way…"

"Just don't ram his car to get his attention like the first time."

I can hear the smile in her voice. "I told you that was an accident, smartass. I'll think of something. Thanks, Eve, I appreciate the pep talk."

"Let me know how it turns out."

"I will. Love you."

"Love you too."

I hang up and hug a throw pillow to my chest, my eyes watering. If I can make up with Eve after years apart, surely I can make up with Eli. My sister met me halfway though. I'm not sure I'll get the same reception from Eli after bailing on him twice.

First things first, time to make peace with Sydney.

~

I get dressed and go straight to The Horseman Inn. It's just before the restaurant opens for dinner, which means they're closed, but the workers are inside preparing. I knock on the door.

A moment later, Sydney looks at me through the glass, her expression hard.

I break out into a cold sweat.

She opens the door. "What?"

"I need to talk to you and explain. Please just hear me out."

She gestures for me to follow her. We settle at a corner table in the front room. The only other people in here are the bartender, Betsy, getting set up behind the bar, and a busboy mopping the back dining room.

"First, I'm really sorry I didn't tell you for so long," I say. "In the beginning, it was so new and fragile. My first serious relationship." My voice cracks. "I didn't expect that. Eli sort of sprang up on me." I blink back tears. "He kidnapped me for a weekend getaway for our first date so we could get to know each other."

"What! He kidnapped you?"

"Yeah, it was crazy. He handcuffed me and everything and carried me out to his car. Next thing I know, we're speeding out of town on our way to New Hampshire."

She leans back in her chair, shaking her head. "Just when I think he's on the straight and narrow, he pulls something like this. So you're telling me he was the instigator of all this."

"I don't want to put it all on him. I was drawn to him from the moment we had our fender bender, but I wasn't going to do anything about it because you warned me off, and part of me agreed, I was too damaged to have a relationship. I thought he'd only get hurt in the end, and I could never do casual with someone I've known most of my life—"

"Not to mention you'd have to see him around town."

"Exactly, but, Syd, he made it so easy. He's so warm and fun. He was everything I needed when I needed it, and somehow I found a way to meet him halfway."

She frowns. "Audrey knew."

I grab her arm. "I wasn't trying to exclude you. Well, I was, but only so I wouldn't lose you in the process. Anyway, Audrey is the one who helped him kidnap me. She said the only way he could get to know me was if we were away together for an extended time."

"Huh." She cocks her head. "She might've been right about that."

"She was!"

She shakes her head. "I'm still pissed I'm the last to know."

"I swear I'll never keep another secret from you again. And I do have feelings for him. Deep feelings. I love him." I bite my trembling lower lip. "I haven't even told him that yet."

She gasps.

I nod, my vision blurring through tears. "It's true. Can you believe it finally happened for me? I don't think it would've happened for anyone else ever. Eli was just safe enough, just persistent enough, just...everything I ever wanted."

"Jenna! Oh my God!" She throws her arms around me in a hug. "My little brother cured you of your awful relationship history!"

I pull back. "Not so little anymore."

She smiles. "You're right. I screwed up. I love you, and I

should've been more supportive. I just didn't realize you had real feelings for him, but that's not the point. I'm sorry."

"I'm sorry too."

She sighs. "I need to let go a bit more where Eli and Caleb are concerned. I still make Caleb text me when he travels for work so I know he arrived safely."

I nudge her shoulder. "Just don't get involved in his love life."

She lifts her palms. "I've learned my lesson. Besides, Caleb has no interest in a relationship. I feel more sorry for the women who fall for him." She grabs my hands, her voice fierce. "I'm so sorry this came between us. I was being way too overprotective. You did the right thing going behind my back because otherwise I would've been all over you, stomping on your little fledgling seedling of a relationship, and now it bloomed into love. That's all I ever wanted for him. For both of you. I just didn't know you wanted that for yourself."

"I do now. Eli wanted to tell you about us, he insisted on it, and I kept saying I would and put it off. I was so scared of losing you."

"I was an idiot," she says magnanimously.

I smile. "If you're okay with it, I'd like to try to get back together with him. We broke up, and then he tried to make up, and I was too upset about you and me—"

"Go! Please, get out of here and win your man back." She stands and gestures broadly for me to leave.

I stand, a little uncertain. "I'm not sure how to do that exactly."

She gives me a little shove. "Tell him you love him. That's the important part."

I walk out, feeling much lighter than when I walked in.

But on the drive home, my thoughts are tangled, going round and round about what made me and Eli break up twice and how to keep it from happening again. Two things stand out—he looked up to me as his ideal dream girl, which I can never live up to, and the terror I have of repeating my parents' mistakes. I need to put us on even footing first and then prove that my love is true.

After my long talk with Eve this weekend, I think I know how to do that.

The next day, I show up at Dr. Russo's office. This may be the strangest plan anyone's come up with to win someone back, but it feels right. I tell the receptionist what I'm there for and wait. I haven't met Dr. Russo since he moved to town last year. I was too busy building my business.

A short while later, Dr. Russo steps out to the waiting room, wearing blue scrubs. He's young, maybe thirty, with thick brown hair and a trimmed beard. He offers his hand. "Hi, I'm Dr. Russo. Good to meet you, Jenna. We're at the early stages of a shelter, so only a few options to choose from. Follow me."

That's right, I'm at the vet's. I saw his listings on a pet rescue site online and filled out an adoption application. I never let myself get a dog before because of the pain of losing one again. This is me moving forward optimistically for the future. Eli had mentioned Dr. Russo wanted to build a shelter, and it seems he's gotten a good start. I follow him to a back room with a few large kennels for dogs and some smaller ones higher up for cats.

He gestures to a small kennel. "We've got a mother-daughter calico cat pairing. Both very gentle."

I look in on the cats. They're curled up together sleeping. "I imagine they'd want to stay together."

"Either way as long as they're both placed in a good home. Have you had a cat before?"

"No. I had a dog once. Actually, I know that's what I want." I walk over to the dogs and kneel to peer into their kennels. One is a black and white dog with pointy ears. He's asleep and opens his eyes briefly when I say hello.

"That guy is a senior," Dr. Russo says. "He's very mellow,

as you can see. Boston terrier. I've been calling him PJ, but I'm not sure if it'll stick."

I turn to the other dog. He's a small brown pit bull standing in the back of his kennel. This is the one I was hoping for from the online listing. A friend for Lucy. "C'mere, doggy. Come a little closer."

The dog looks wary.

Dr. Russo hands me a biscuit. "I call him Mocha because of his brown coat."

I smile. "That's great because I'm a baker. Mocha is a great flavor." I offer the treat through the bars. "A treat for you! You know you want it."

Mocha sniffs the air and slowly approaches.

"Just a little closer," I coax.

He takes the treat with a snap, and I yank my hand back. He takes the biscuit to the corner, turning his back on us to enjoy it.

Dr. Russo gestures toward him. "He's about nine months old. Neutered, up to date on shots, but he hasn't had much human interaction. It will take time and patience to get him comfortable with social contact."

I stand. "I'll take him."

He flashes a smile. "Maybe you should interact a little more closely first. I'll put him on a leash, and you can take a walk together, sound good?"

I nod, but I already know. This is my dog. He's a little broken, but nothing that a lot of loving can't fix. Just like me.

Dr. Russo opens the kennel and coaxes Mocha out with another treat, clipping a leash to his harness. "Fair warning, he's strong and not well trained, so the harness is better on walks. It won't pull at his neck, choking him."

"Got it."

He hands me a few treats from his pocket. "In case you need to coax him. Besides, it'll make you smell very good to him."

I tuck the treats into my fleece jacket pocket, take the leash, and feed Mocha a treat. "Walk time!" I try to sound upbeat and positive so he won't be scared.

Mocha follows docilely behind me until I open the door of the room, and then he bolts forward, yanking my arm. I laugh and hurry up so he doesn't pull my arm from its socket. "Wait for me!"

"Gather more leash in your hand!" Dr. Russo yells. "Don't give him too much lead."

Mocha halts at the glass front door of the vet's office and paws at it. I wind the leash around my hand for a better grip, making sure it's in a spot for maximum leverage for me. I whisper to Mocha, "We're going to take a short walk down the street and back. We have to prove we can do this together. Ready?"

He paws the door. I just know he's going to bolt again.

"Can you sit?" I hold the treat above his head. He leaps and grabs it, chomping it down.

Dr. Russo laughs behind us. "I can recommend a trainer to help you with him."

I smile at him. "I'll be taking you up on that." I turn to Mocha. "Slowly," I order.

He looks at me, then the door, then me.

I open it, and he lunges forward. I dig my heels in, gaining control. "Here we go, nice and easy." I walk at a brisk pace, Mocha trotting beside me, looking thrilled to be outside. He pulls to the side, and I let him sniff a Stop sign. He pees next to it, and then he sniffs the grass all around it. Probably a popular pee spot close to the vet's office.

"Okay, let's keep going." I give the leash a tug, and we continue our walk. I'm half pulling him back to me while he pulls forward, urging me to catch up with him. It's not easy, but I'm happy. I think with time we'll learn to work together.

I circle us back and head toward the vet's office. Mocha keeps pulling until we reach the parking lot and then halts, digging his heels in. He thinks he's going back in the kennel.

I stop and crouch next to him. "I'd like to take you home with me, and then you'll never have to be at the vet's again except for checkups, but then I'll bring you right back out. So this is just a visit. I'm going to adopt you. Would you like that?"

He sniffs my jacket pocket and manages to get his nose in it, snagging the last of my treats. His muzzle gets caught on the fleece fabric, and he shakes his head to get free. I laugh, peeling it off him. He licks my hand, wagging his tail. I think he likes me.

I stand. "Okay, let's go."

I tug him forward with some effort toward the door, and Dr. Russo holds the door open for us. "He didn't want to come back."

Dr. Russo grins. "They never do. Vets give them shots and poke them too much."

"It wasn't an easy walk, but I think it went well. He licked my hand."

"He's all yours. Let me get his paperwork and enough dog food to get you started. Congratulations! You're a dog mom." He whips a cap from behind his back and hands it to me. It says Dog Mom.

My heart squeezes, warmth rushing through me. I'm a mom. Well, the canine variety, but still. It makes me feel good to have this loving responsibility.

I put the cap on. "This is adorable! What a great idea."

"Thanks, yeah, it was part of our fundraiser for the shelter, and I thought it would be good to give them out to our adopters. We couldn't do this without people like you."

"I'm thrilled to do it."

I pet Mocha while I wait for the paperwork. He's standing, his eyes glued to the front door. I'm already in love with him. I never expected to have such an instant connection. My original thought was that adopting a dog would show Eli I could get over past hurts, like when my parents gave away my dog, so he'd give me a second chance. And now it turns out I was really healing me.

Mocha yanks the leash as he bolts for the front door, and it slips from my hand. I rush to catch up with him. "Not yet. You like your food, right? Dr. Russo is coming back with it."

I tug him back farther into the waiting room. He flops down at my feet, resting his head on his paws, giving me the big puppy-dog eyes. This is going to be a lot of work. A lot of loving.

I can't wait.

I found out when Eli had off work and got my assistant to cover my shift, so I could finally make my move. It's Saturday, three days after adopting Mocha. I needed to get him settled in before taking him somewhere. He's in the back seat of my car. I figure I'll introduce him to Lucy outside, in case Lucy isn't happy with another dog in her house. Eli will see how hard I'm trying to move forward, and then I'll ask him for a second chance. Oh, and I got him roses with a note of my own. Just like he did all those years ago.

I ring the bell, the flowers hidden behind my back, adrenaline racing through me.

Caleb answers with Lucy barking at his side. "Hey, Jenna." He turns to Lucy. "Sit."

She sits, and I reach out with my hand for her to sniff. She goes crazy sniffing me, probably because of Mocha.

"Is Eli around?" I ask.

"Yeah, come in. He's upstairs, probably moping again. You broke his heart, you know."

I grimace. Caleb always says what he thinks. "It was mutual. Should I just go up?" I pull the roses from behind my back and tuck them into the crook of my arm.

He stares at them. "Uh, he needs some warning. You don't just spring up on a mopey guy. What if he's in there playing some weepy song on guitar? Too embarrassing." He goes to the stairs and yells, "Eli! You got company!"

No response.

He shakes his head and goes upstairs, knocking on his door. I follow him most of the way upstairs, eavesdropping shamelessly.

"What?" Eli asks.

"You got company. It's a mopey-looking woman with roses."

There's a scuffle, and then Eli appears. "Jenna."

Caleb moves on to his room and shuts the door, giving us privacy.

"Hi," I say, my heart pounding.

He searches my expression. "Hi. Let's go downstairs."

I head downstairs on shaky legs. The moment we're in the living room, I thrust the roses at him. "I missed you. There's a note."

He pulls the note from the small envelope and reads it. Then he grabs me with his free arm and crushes me to him. "Jenna."

I wrap my arms around his middle, hugging him for a long moment, my heart thudding hard. I look up at him, emotion clogging my throat. "I mean it. I love you, Eli."

He cradles my jaw, his face flushed, his eyes watering. "This is exactly what I wrote in your note all those years ago." He sets the roses on the coffee table and holds up the card with my three little words that encompass so much feeling—I love you.

My jaw gapes. "That's what you wrote when you were sixteen? That was so brave of you!"

"As embarrassing as it is to admit, it's true." He tucks the note in his back pocket, frames my face with both hands, and kisses me tenderly. "I love you. Still, always."

Warmth spreads through my chest, my limbs light. It's pure happiness like I've never felt before. This is a man who knows my strengths and flaws, and loves all of me. He holds me close, and I sigh, wrapped in pure happiness and so much love. We stay like that for a long time. I can't stop smiling. I'm just so happy to be together again.

He pulls away and gazes deep into my eyes with so much love I wonder how I didn't see it before. I feel energized like I could just spontaneously break out into square dancing. Ha! Instead I kiss him.

I run my fingers through the hair at the nape of his neck. "I would've been shocked at a declaration of love back then."

His lips curve up in a small smile. "It was premature but heartfelt. I'm sorry for having such a chip on my shoulder about me being the adoring one for so long. I should've just started from scratch the moment we reconnected as adults and forgot all that other stuff."

"It was nice in a way. A lot to live up to but nice."

He strokes my hair back from my face. "I don't want you to feel like you have to live up to some fantasy version of you I built up in my mind. I love who you are right now."

"That's a relief because I'm far from perfect."

"Neither am I. Besides, most of my dream-girl fantasies were of the dirty variety, and you've far surpassed all expectations."

I laugh. "That's good to hear. How long were you having these dirty fantasies?"

He grins. "You don't want to know."

I take a deep breath. "I had a heart-to-heart with Sydney, and she's good with me, with us too. I confessed everything, including how much I love you. That's all she ever wanted for you."

"I know. She got out of line though."

I pull away. "Well, she admitted her mistake and apologized. I do have one other thing I need to say."

He inclines his head, his eyes intent on mine.

"I needed to open my heart again and—" I squeak as Lucy's head pops up between my legs. I push her back, and she nudges my hand for pets. I stroke her head, feeling calmer. "I'm working really hard on healing and being more open. In fact, I have someone waiting to meet you outside."

His brows scrunch together as he cocks his head to the side. "You do?"

"Yes. Make sure Lucy stays here. I'm not sure how she'll react."

I head outside, and he follows. Then I go to the back seat, and Mocha's head pops out the window with a happy bark. He's bonded with me, but he's still unsure about other people. I open the door, grabbing his leash before I undo his seatbelt. He leaps out of the car and races around me. I hold him tight and tell him to sit.

Mocha suddenly notices Eli and retreats, standing behind me.

"This is Mocha," I say. "I adopted him because I was trying to get over one of my past hurts from my parents giving away my beloved dog. Even though I love dogs, I never let myself get one as an adult because I couldn't bear the idea of losing the dog again. I know it's not logical, but...anyway, I'm trying to heal and move forward. Mocha here is helping me."

"That's great. I'm glad to hear it." He kisses me and cups my jaw, gazing into my eyes. "I love that you did this."

Mocha barks.

I turn around to look at him. "It's okay. He's my people."

Eli crouches down and offers his hand for Mocha to sniff. I give Eli a treat to offer Mocha, who takes it and allows Eli to pet him. Progress. Of course Mocha would trust Eli. He's a great guy.

Eli looks up at me. "He's still a pup."

"Dr. Russo says he's nine months old. He's very playful once he gets comfortable."

He stands, smiling at me. "Should we introduce him to Lucy?"

I beam. "We should. After all, they could be roommates one day."

"Roommates, huh?"

"Mocha could be for both of us because I hope we're always going to be together."

He searches my expression. "Have your feelings changed on marriage?"

I suck in air, alarmed.

"I'm not proposing, just asking if your feelings changed."

I think about the progress I'm making with Mocha as a dog mom. I love having someone to take care of. "I do think kids would be nice one day."

"Okay, kids." He strokes my cheek. "I like that answer."

I hold up a palm. "I would only ever consider marriage with you, but don't propose. We should be together for a year at least just to be sure."

He kisses me. "I'm in no rush."

I relax. And then I smile so big my cheeks hurt. "I'm ridiculously happy. I can't stop smiling."

He laughs. "Me too. Let me get Lucy out here to introduce our new family member."

Happiness bubbles up inside me, making me feel light and floaty. *Our family*.

A moment later, Lucy bounds out of the house with Eli, and Mocha cowers behind me.

Eli makes Lucy sit, and I draw Mocha over, giving both dogs treats. Lucy moves to sniff Mocha, who stands very stiff and still. After she sniffs him, she makes a play bow. Mocha looks uncertain.

"That's a good start," Eli says. "She wants to play. Let's bring them inside and let them play with the stuff in her toy basket."

I follow him in. Mocha sniffs around the perimeter of the room while Lucy takes out toy after toy, dropping them near Mocha.

"I think she'll teach him to chill," I say. "Maybe she'll be like a third mom to him."

"Third?"

"There's his canine mom, and then me, his second mom. I have the hat to prove it. It says Dog Mom right on there."

"Sounds official," he teases, tugging a lock of my hair. "You must've been at Dr. Russo's place."

Lucy barks, and Mocha finally lifts his head from his sniff-ing-the-room adventure. Then he notices the large rubber figure-eight toy Lucy dropped next to him. He gingerly takes it and then settles down to chew. Lucy grabs her orange fireman hose toy and settles next to him.

"While they're busy, maybe we could..." Eli points upstairs.

"Caleb's here," I whisper.

"Yo, Caleb!" he yells.

A moment later, Caleb appears, jogging downstairs. "I know, I know. I'll spend the night at Drew's place. We've got work tomorrow morning anyway." He works at the dojo with him part time when he's not doing his modeling thing.

Eli takes my hand and walks with me upstairs. "When did you realize you loved me?"

"I feel like I've always loved you."

"You did not love me when we were kids."

"I always had a soft spot for you. You had a sense of fun and mischief I always liked."

We reach his room, but he stops me, his hands on my hips. "What about as adults?"

My mind flashes back to all the things Eli has shown me—the small gestures, the tenderness, the gruff care. "I'd say it was when you kidnapped me. I thought, here's a guy who cares so much about me, he takes me away from it all just to get to know me better."

"Hmm…one could argue that wasn't exactly romantic. And I handcuffed you."

"Because you understood I needed a push. Taking sex off the table was a genius move. No guy has ever done that before. Though it was pretty much a done deal once we kissed."

He kisses me, smiling against my lips. "I've adored you my entire life, but the moment it tripped into real love was when I saw you look longingly at General Joan's great-granddaughter's baby picture. I saw the love you were capable of and knew I had to have it for myself. My heart fell that day and will keep falling, every day for the rest of my life."

"Oh, Eli." I throw my arms around him and kiss him passionately.

We stumble through the doorway together.

I hear the door slam behind me, and then there's nothing but fiery heat and real, true love.

EPILOGUE

Eli

It's the Saturday after Thanksgiving, and I'm playing guitar at The Horseman Inn. I invited Jenna to Thanksgiving with my family, which was at Sydney and Wyatt's house this year. That was the only place big enough for our growing family. Wyatt and Sydney invited his mom and three sisters, plus me and my three brothers. It was a little crazy with all the people and dogs. I told Wyatt we should start a puppy bowl and let the dogs play their own version of football with dog toys. He wouldn't go for it because he felt his little shih tzu, Snowball, would be at a disadvantage. Probably right. Especially compared to the competition. Wyatt and Sydney have a pit bull mix, Jenna and I have two pit bulls, my brother Adam has an English bulldog, and Caleb just adopted a Siberian husky that came into the shelter. All much bigger and stronger than little Snowball.

Jenna and I stopped in at her dad's condo, where her mom is now living, for Thanksgiving dessert. Yup, after all that drama, Jenna's parents are back together again, not married, but they seem happy. Jenna's sister, Eve, was there too, who's trying to make peace with her family. I guess some couples can't help being drawn to each other over and over, even if they don't know how to make the marriage part work. I say whatever works for them. Just don't put Jenna in the middle of it.

I'm playing Aerosmith's "I Don't Want to Miss a Thing" at Jenna's request. It's our song. She's sitting at the table closest to me, looking like my biggest fan. I swear she looks more beautiful every day. Her blond hair just brushes the shoulders of her long-sleeved beige sweater dress that clings to her sexy body, ending mid-thigh. Of course, it's not just her hair, clothes, or body that makes her glow with natural beauty. It's because she's in love. She's smiling at me, her green eyes sparkling, a rosy pink to her cheeks.

I smile back and hold her gaze. *I love you*, I mouth.

"Love you too," she whispers.

She invited family and friends here tonight, too, including her parents and sister. Actually, this is the biggest crowd I've ever seen for the Saturday after Thanksgiving. The back dining room is standing room only with all of our family and friends.

I finish the song to enthusiastic applause.

Jenna stands and throws something into my open guitar case. I pick it up. Strange. It's a picture from Sydney's birthday party when I was seven and Jenna was nine. The girls are gathered close, smiling. I'm behind Jenna, making bunny ears.

I laugh. "This is awesome."

Sydney pipes up. "I found it in an old photo album." The two of them are closer than ever. I just keep hearing "sisters" over and over. My sister is giddy over Jenna being part of the family. Well, not officially, but…

Jenna drops another item into my guitar case. It's a rubber treat dispenser toy for dogs.

My brows lift in question. It's not like the dogs are here with us.

Jenna smiles impishly and tosses another item in. I pick up a small card with a recipe for the maple whiskey cider drink we had at the lodge in New Hampshire. Rye whiskey, maple syrup, lemon, and apple cider. Okay, I guess she wants to make it here. These little gifts feel like a trip down memory lane, except for the new dog toy.

Jenna closes the distance, pulls her hand from behind her back, and drops a blue garter belt into the case.

My heart kicks harder. *That* is a wedding thing.

Suddenly Jenna's on one knee next to my chair. I set my guitar in its case so I can give her my full attention.

"Did you guess?" she whispers. "I gave you something old, something new, something borrowed, something blue. I'm in love with you, Eli, and I want to spend the rest of my life with you. Will you marry me?"

My eyes water. I can't believe she did this. "I'm speechless."

"Answer her!" someone yells.

I suddenly realize this is why she invited all of our family and friends here tonight. She wanted to share our engagement publicly, everything out in the open.

"Yes, of course I will." I scoop her up off the floor and hug her tight. "Jenna, my love."

I pull back to look at her and wipe tears from her cheeks. "You really surprised me. You said we should wait a year."

"That was scared Jenna talking." She pulls a diamond engagement ring from the pocket of her dress. "This is *completely and totally in love, never looking back* Jenna." She puts the ring on. "I picked out what I would like."

"Now what am I supposed to do with the diamond ring sitting at my house?"

She gasps and throws her arms around my neck. "I would've said yes if you got there first."

"Of course you would. I'm irresistible." I kiss her.

The crowd erupts in applause, and I hear the pop of champagne. Next thing I know, everyone's gathered close, congratulating us.

Audrey beams at us. "Congratulations, you two! I'm so happy for you. And I like to think I played a small part in helping you get together."

I hug Audrey. "Thanks for being on my side."

She smiles. "I was on both your sides. I just knew it was a match."

Jenna pulls her ring off and offers it to Audrey. "Could you hang onto this for safekeeping until I can return it? It turns out Eli already got me a ring. I want him to put his ring on me for the official ring."

Audrey stares at the ring like it's a snake. "Uh...can't you put it in your purse?"

"I know it sounds superstitious, but I feel like I should only have the official one."

Audrey stuffs it in her purse, her gaze darting around, like she's hiding something dangerous.

"You can wear it if you want," Jenna says.

Audrey shakes her head vigorously. "No, no. That wouldn't be right. I'll hang onto it until you can return it."

"Next week."

"Got it," Audrey says, standing stiffly like she's on guard. "It's important you feel comfortable with your engagement."

Wyatt's sister Paige leans over from where she was talking to Brooke and Sydney. "Actually, they don't usually accept returns on engagement rings, or they'll give you only a partial refund. Ask me how I know."

"Can I wear your old ring to keep guys away?" Brooke asks Paige. "I'm tired of attracting the worst of the male species."

Paige shrugs. "Sure, why not? Just don't lose it."

Brooke scoffs. "You trusted Kayla to wear it for a whole summer while she played the fake engagement game."

"I trust you. I told her not to lose it too."

They walk off together, bickering like siblings do. Brooke seems to have completely forgotten she was offered up as my date. Never would've worked. My heart was already taken.

Caleb appears by my side and can't help but gloat. "Looks like my extremely wise advice worked. I told you to back off and she'd come to you."

"Actually," Jenna starts.

I cut her off before she can share how I chased her. "It wasn't your advice. I let her know I was into her. Maybe you should try it, and you'd actually have something real for once."

Caleb claps me on the shoulder. "I'm too young to settle down, old man."

"You're two years younger than me."

Jenna smiles serenely. "Age doesn't mean much when it comes to love."

Caleb shakes his head. "Only love I have is for Huckleberry." That's his new husky, two years old, and a happy guy just like his owner.

"At least call him Huck," a feminine voice says. "The other dogs will make fun of him for such a goofy name."

We turn to find Sloane, the mechanic who fixed my car. She's sitting at the end of the bar.

Caleb walks over, already defending his choice in name.

Sloane turns from him, dismissing his impassioned argument.

He says something to her, charmer smile in place, probably asking to buy her a drink.

She shakes her head, tosses some cash on the bar, and walks out the door.

Caleb stares after her.

"That might be the first time a woman ever walked away from him," I say under my breath.

"That looked painful," Jenna whispers. "I'm glad I'm not out in the wilds of dating land anymore."

I tuck a lock of her silky hair behind her ear. "Now you're in the wilds of Eli land."

"When did you buy me an engagement ring?"

"The day after you gave me roses, I knew you were it for me. I was just waiting for the right time. I thought about Christmas Eve, maybe kiss you under the mistletoe, and then slide it on your finger with a proposal."

She smiles. "You were awfully confident I'd say yes. Just slide it on before my answer."

"It was my workaround for your waiting-a-year thing. Just do it quick."

She laughs.

"And you must've been confident too. You invited everyone we know to witness it." I cup her jaw and kiss her. "I guess we both knew it was right. There honestly wasn't a single doubt in my mind."

"Mine either. Can we go back to your place for the ring you picked out?"

"Absolutely."

We walk out the door together, hand in hand, our friends and family whistling and cheering for us.

Once we get to the quiet parking lot on this clear moonlit night, I turn to her. "They probably think we're about to—"

"Plan our future together."

"I was going to say rip each other's clothes off. Let's plan to buy a place together as soon as we find one in Summerdale we both like. You can move in with me in the meantime."

"What about Caleb?"

"Maybe he could take your apartment while we take the house. After all, there's two of us *and* two dogs. That's like a family right there. We need room to spread out in a house with a yard."

"If he's okay with it, I am."

We walk to my Mustang, the silver glowing in the moonlight. She's a thing of beauty, maybe even more so now that she's imperfect in the bumper. It's a happy reminder of how I reconnected with Jenna.

I turn to her. "What do you think of a New Year's Eve wedding? Something small."

She throws her arms around my neck. "Yes. I love that idea. Small and intimate, nothing too fancy. And then we can start our new life together with the New Year."

"Kids whenever you're ready. I'm looking forward to being a dad. My own dad set a great example."

She wipes her eyes. "All this time I had all this fear built up over what a committed relationship means, but with you all I feel is happiness."

"Then why're you crying?"

"Happy tears!"

I nuzzle into her neck, breathing her in. "I didn't know Jenna Larsen ever had that kind."

She pushes at my chest. "Well, I do now, thanks to you."

I grin. "You're welcome."

Her lips meet mine in a passionate kiss that ignites way too hot for a parking lot. I break the kiss. "Come on, I need to get you home."

"Yes, home."

It's never sounded sweeter.

Don't miss the next book in the series, *Toying*, where Caleb gets hit by a thunderbolt of love!

Toying

When the male model meets the female mechanic, get ready for a thunderbolt!

Sloane

When you're told you're the ugly duckling, you learn to set your expectations low. So what do I do when Caleb Robinson, a gorgeous model, offers to buy me a drink? I turn him down flat. It must be a prank.

Two days later, I'm working at the garage in my dirty blue coveralls with grease smudged on my face, and he shows up to ask again. I'm *floored*. What's this guy up to? Men like him don't date girls like me.

Caleb

I'm in full-on pursuit of the coolest woman ever, who's destined to be my wife—Sloane Murray. Dad always said that's how it happened for him. He proposed to Mom on their first date. I never believed love could happen so quickly, until now.

Slowly but surely, I convince Sloane of my sincerity, and our future has hope until I bring her into my modeling world. Problem is, she doesn't fit. And when my career takes off, it's clear that I can't pursue the big dream and my dream girl. If only love was as simple as that first thunderbolt.

ALSO BY KYLIE GILMORE

Unleashed Romance <<steamy romcoms with dogs!

Fetching (Book 1)

Dashing (Book 2)

Sporting (Book 3)

Toying (Book 4)

Blazing (Book 5)

The Clover Park Series <<brothers who put family first!

The Opposite of Wild (Book 1)

Daisy Does It All (Book 2)

Bad Taste in Men (Book 3)

Kissing Santa (Book 4)

Restless Harmony (Book 5)

Not My Romeo (Book 6)

Rev Me Up (Book 7)

An Ambitious Engagement (Book 8)

Clutch Player (Book 9)

A Tempting Friendship (Book 10)

Clover Park Bride: Nico and Lily's Wedding

A Valentine's Day Gift (Book 11)

Maggie Meets Her Match (Book 12)

The Clover Park STUDS series <<hawt geeks who unleash into studs!

Almost Over It (Book 1)

Almost Married (Book 2)

Almost Fate (Book 3)

Almost in Love (Book 4)

Almost Romance (Book 5)

Almost Hitched (Book 6)

Happy Endings Book Club Series <<the Campbell family and a romance book club collide!

Hidden Hollywood (Book 1)

Inviting Trouble (Book 2)

So Revealing (Book 3)

Formal Arrangement (Book 4)

Bad Boy Done Wrong (Book 5)

Mess With Me (Book 6)

Resisting Fate (Book 7)

Chance of Romance (Book 8)

Wicked Flirt (Book 9)

An Inconvenient Plan (Book 10)

A Happy Endings Wedding (Book 11)

The Rourkes Series <<swoonworthy princes and kickass princesses!

Royal Catch (Book 1)

Royal Hottie (Book 2)

Royal Darling (Book 3)

Royal Charmer (Book 4)

Royal Player (Book 5)

Royal Shark (Book 6)

Rogue Prince (Book 7)

Rogue Gentleman (Book 8)

Rogue Rascal (Book 9)

Rogue Angel (Book 10)

Rogue Devil (Book 11)

Rogue Beast (Book 12)

Check out my website for the most up-to-date list of my books: kyliegilmore.com/books

ABOUT THE AUTHOR

Kylie Gilmore is the *USA Today* bestselling author of the Unleashed Romance series, the Rourkes series, the Happy Endings Book Club series, the Clover Park series, and the Clover Park STUDS series. She writes humorous romance that makes you laugh, cry, and reach for a cold glass of water.

Kylie lives in New York with her family, two cats, and a nutso dog. When she's not writing, reading hot romance, or dutifully taking notes at writing conferences, you can find her flexing her muscles all the way to the high cabinet for her secret chocolate stash.

Sign up for Kylie's Newsletter and get a FREE book! kyliegilmore.com/newsletter

For text alerts on Kylie's new releases, text KYLIE to the number 21000. (US only)

For more fun stuff check out Kylie's website https://www.kyliegilmore.com.

Thanks for reading *Sporting*. I hope you enjoyed it. Would you like to know about new releases? You can sign up for my new release email list at kyliegilmore.com/newsletter. I promise not to clog your inbox! Only new release info, sales, and some fun giveaways.

I love to hear from readers! You can find me at:

kyliegilmore.com
Instagram.com/kyliegilmore
Facebook.com/KylieGilmoreToo
Twitter @KylieGilmoreToo

If you liked Eli and Jenna's story, please leave a review on your favorite retailer's website or Goodreads. Thank you.

Made in the USA
Columbia, SC
26 August 2021

44417173R00102